KU-538-669

M. C. Beaton is the author of both the Agatha Raisin and Hamish Macbeth series, as well as numerous Regency romances. Her Agatha Raisin books have been turned into a TV series on Sky 1. She lives in Paris and in a Cotswolds village that is very much like Agatha's beloved Carsely.

The Hamish Macbeth series

DEATH OF A TRAVELLING MAN

A HAMISH MACBETH MURDER MYSTERY

M.C. BEATON

Constable • London

CONSTABLE

First published in the United States in 1993 by Ballantine Books,
a division of Random House, 1745 Broadway, New York, NY 10019

First published in the UK in 2009 by Robinson,
an imprint of Constable & Robinson Ltd.

This edition published in Great Britain in 2017 by Constable

1 3 5 7 9 10 8 6 4 2

Copyright © M. C. Beaton, 1993, 2009

The moral right of the author has been asserted.

*All characters and events in this publication, other than
those clearly in the public domain, are fictitious
and any resemblance to real persons,
living or dead, is purely coincidental.*

All rights reserved.
No part of this publication may be reproduced, stored in a retrieval
system, or transmitted, in any form, or by any means, without the
prior permission in writing of the publisher, nor be otherwise
circulated in any form of binding or cover other than that in which
it is published and without a similar condition including this
condition being imposed on the subsequent purchaser.

A CIP catalogue record for this book
is available from the British Library.

ISBN: 978-1-47212-445-6

Typeset in Palatino by Photoprint
Printed and bound in Great Britain by
CPI Group (UK) Ltd, Croydon CR0 4YY

Papers used by Constable are from well-managed forests and other
responsible sources.

Constable
An imprint of
Little, Brown Book Group
Carmelite House
50 Victoria Embankment
London EC4Y 0DZ

An Hachette UK Company
www.hachette.co.uk

www.littlebrown.co.uk

To Sacha Moore,
with love

Chapter One

From his brimstone bed, at break of day,
A-walking the Devil is gone,
To look at his little snug farm of the World,
And see how his stock went on.
                                    – Robert Southey

Police Sergeant Hamish Macbeth was never to forget that fine spring day.

It was the day the devil came to Lochdubh.

Hamish was strolling along the waterfront of the tiny Highland village, glad to be free for a brief spell from the bloodhound efficiency of his sidekick, PC Willie Lamont. Although his promotion to sergeant had meant more pay, it had also meant that this eager beaver of a policeman had been thrust upon him, interfering with Hamish's easygoing life and home. Willie was also a cleanliness fanatic and Hamish was tired of living with the all-pervading smell of disinfectant.

1

The day was fine and warm, unusual for March in the Highlands. Snow glittered on the twin peaks of the mountains which soared above the village, and the sea loch lay calm and placid in the morning sun. Peat smoke rose from cottage chimneys, seagulls swooped and dived.

And then Hamish saw it, parked in front of what was once the Lochdubh Hotel, still up for sale. It was a battered old bus which had been converted into a travelling home. At one time in its career the bus had been painted psyche-delic colours but even these had faded into pastel streaks overlaid with brown trails of rust.

Hamish went up to it and knocked at the door. The door jerked open. A tall man smiled down at Hamish. He was incredibly hand-some. Jet black hair grew to a widow's peak on his forehead. His eyes were green, grass-green without a fleck of brown in them. His face and arms were tanned golden-brown. He was wearing a blue-and-white checked shirt and blue jeans moulded to long muscular legs.

'You are not allowed to park here,' said Hamish, wondering why he should take such an instant and violent dislike to this handsome man.

'I am a traveller,' the man said in a cultivated English voice. 'My name is Sean Gourlay.'

Hamish's face hardened. Sean would have

been called a hippie not so long ago and a beatnik a long time before that. Now he belonged to that unlovable crowd who euphemistically referred to themselves as travellers, the itinerant race who descended on places like Stonehenge complete with battered unlicensed vehicles, dirt, drugs and dogs. To some charitable souls who had never had their sheep ripped apart by dogs or their land turned into a sewer, the travellers carried with them an aura of romance, like the gypsies they pretended to be. Living on the dole, they travelled aimlessly from place to place. The reason these nomadic layabouts claimed to be 'travellers' or sometimes 'new travellers' was that they demanded the privileges and camping rights given to gypsies, privileges often dating back centuries. Hamish was tolerant of gypsies and knew them all. He had no time for these so-called travellers.

'You are not a gypsy,' said Hamish, 'and therefore have no rights. This is private property.'

A girl squeezed in beside Sean at the doorway. She had straggly sun-bleached hair, a small dirty face, and a thin, flat-chested body.

'Get lost, pig,' she said, in the guttural accents of Glasgow.

Hamish ignored her. He addressed himself to Sean. 'I can direct you to a place up on the moors where you can camp.'

3

Sean gave him a blinding smile. 'But I like this village,' he said.

'And so do I,' retorted Hamish, 'which is why I am ordering you to move on. Let's see your driving licence.'

A stream of four-letter words erupted from the girl. Sean dug into the back pocket of his jeans and produced a clean new driving licence, issued only a few months ago. The girl had now jumped down from the bus. She was very small in stature. She leapt up and down in front of Hamish, cursing and yelling. 'Pig' was the politest epithet. There was a peculiar, almost sinister magnetism about Sean. He paid no attention to the girl whatsoever and Hamish found himself doing the same. He examined Sean's insurance and the road-tax disc on the bus. Both were in order.

He handed back the papers and said firmly, 'Now, get moving.'

Sean grinned. 'Certainly, officer.'

The girl told Hamish to perform an impossible anatomical act on himself and then suddenly bolted back into the bus, like some small hairy animal darting into its lair.

'Pay no attention to Cheryl,' said Sean lazily. 'Rather an excitable type.'

'Her full name?' snapped Hamish.

'Cheryl Higgins, like the professor.'

Hamish waited until Sean had climbed into the driver's seat, and the bus clattered off. He

4

stood with his hands on his hips and watched it go. Then he shook his head. He should not have allowed Sean to upset him. If they parked up on the moors, they would not stay long. He knew the travellers preferred to be with their own kind. It was unusual to find just two of them and one old bus. This fine weather was unusual. Soon there would be the 'lambing blizzard', that last vicious fall of snow which always arrived in the late spring to plague the shepherds.

His mind turned to the problem of PC Willie Lamont. He would not have minded at all having a helper. All policemen, however crime-free the area they lived in, were landed with a lot of paperwork. Hamish regarded the police station as his home, his own home, and he wished he could manage to get Willie to live somewhere else in the village. As he ambled back again in the direction of the police station, he saw that his dog, Towser, was once more tied up in the garden. Poor Towser was always being banished outside these days, thought Hamish. Willie must be scrubbing the floors . . . again. He decided to go up to Tommel Castle Hotel where his friend, Priscilla Halburton-Smythe, was working in the hotel gift shop. Priscilla's father, Colonel Halburton-Smythe, had turned his home into a hotel to recoup the vast losses he had made by trusting his money to a charlatan. The hotel had prospered, having excellent shooting and fishing and high enough charges to appeal to the snobbish and the parvenues who thought the colonel's high-handed manner with his guests was a sign of true breeding, rather than the mixture of arrogance and sheer bloody-mindedness that it, in truth, was.

As he unhitched Towser and led the dog to the police Land Rover, Hamish reflected sadly that having Willie in the police station was like being married to a nag of a wife. Archie Maclean, the fisherman, spent most of his time either in the pub or sitting on the harbour wall to get away from his wife's perpetual cleaning.

The new gift shop was a pleasant place, full of the very best of Scottish goods: Edinburgh crystal, Caithness glass, silver jewellery, fine woollens, along with a multitude of cheaper goods for the tourist to take home – short-bread, locally made fudge, guidebooks, post-cards, souvenir pens and pencils, and stuffed toys.

Priscilla was wearing her new tourist uniform of frilled white shirt and short tartan skirt. Hamish wondered what the tourists made of her, this graceful woman with the smooth blonde hair and the superb figure who looked as if she had stepped out of the pages of *Vogue*.

She saw Hamish and smiled. 'I've had a coffee machine put in here. You must have got word of it.'

'I am not mooching,' said Hamish, who nearly always was. 'But I will have the coffee, nonetheless.'

'What brings you here, Sergeant?' asked Priscilla as she poured two mugs of coffee. She never tired of calling him Sergeant these days, he reflected. He knew she took his promotion as a sign that he had finally come to his senses and decided to be ambitious.

'It's Willie,' he said. 'Cleaning again. I cannae call my house my own.'

'You're too easygoing, Hamish,' said Priscilla firmly. 'You should put your foot down. Find him something to do.'

'Well, I was thinking of phoning the superintendent and pointing out that there is not the work here for two men.'

'And then what would happen?' demanded Priscilla. 'The police station would be closed down and you would be moved to Strathbane and you would hate that. I mean, it's not as if you want to be demoted, is it?'

'As a matter o' fact that waud suit me chust fine,' said Hamish, whose Highland accent became more marked when he was upset. 'I had the good life afore the last murder and I should ha' let Blair take the credit for solving it.' Detective Chief Inspector Blair was the bane of Hamish's life, but in the past he had let him take the credit for solving cases, not wanting any promotion to disturb his calm life. But at the end of the last case, during which Blair had been more than usually obnoxious, Hamish had cracked and told the superintendent that he had solved the case himself and so the result had been promotion to sergeant – and the arrival of Willie.

'Oh, Hamish, you're just saying that.'

'No, I am not. I had the fine life afore I got these wretched stripes. I want Willie and his scrubbing brush out and I don't know how tae go about it.'

She sat down on a high stool behind the counter and crossed her legs. They were excellent legs, thought Hamish not for the first time, but he wasn't going to be daft enough to fall in love with her again. He had enough trouble in his life with Willie.

'Look,' said Priscilla, 'here's something we could do.'

Hamish brightened at the sound of that 'we'. He found another stool and perched on it, facing her over the glass counter. There was a sample bottle of a scent called Mist o' the Highlands. He sprayed some on his hand and sniffed it. It was very strong and very sweet and cloying.

'Pooh,' he said, scrubbing at his hand.

'Can't you leave any free sample alone?' said

Priscilla. 'You'll smell of that stuff for weeks. Believe me, I've tried it. It's immune to soap and water. Now about Willie. He's a bachelor, right?'

'Aye, and likely to remain so,' said Hamish with feeling. 'What woman can compete with all thon cleaning and polishing and cooking? Besides, he's a terribly finicky eater.'

'That doesn't matter. An awful lot of people are finicky eaters, and there are a lot of women who would be delighted to have a house-keeper.'

'What are you getting at?'

'Find him a wife,' said Priscilla. 'If he gets married, there's no room in that station for a married couple. They'd need to find him new quarters.'

Hamish's face brightened. Then it fell. 'Who is there who would even look at the beast?'

'We've got a new hotel receptionist. Doris Ward's her name. Prissy, fussy, competent, not all that good-looking. Invite Willie up to the castle tonight and we'll all have dinner. It'll start his meeting females anyway.'

'All right,' said Hamish. 'I'll try anything.'

He was driving back slowly through the village but he slowed to a mere crawl as he saw a vision standing outside Napoli, the new Italian restaurant. The vision was shaking out a duster. She had an old-fashioned figure, that is, she had a voluptuous bust, a tiny waist and a saucy plump backside. She was wearing a short, skimpy black dress over which was tied a frilly checked apron. She had a heart-shaped face, a tiny nose and a wide soft mouth. Her hair was a riot of dusky curls. She was wearing very high heels and she had firm-muscled calves, like you see on dancer's legs.

Must be one of old Ferrari's relatives, thought Hamish. Mr Ferrari was a Scottish Italian, that is, his father had settled in Scotland at the turn of the century. From his father, Mr Ferrari had inherited a prosperous restaurant in Edinburgh, but having retired and turned it over to his sons, he found time lying heavy on his hands. And so he had started the restaurant in Lochdubh and staffed it with remoter relatives from Italy.

Hamish arrived at the police station in time to meet Willie, who had his uniform on and was preparing to leave.

'Where are you off to?' asked Hamish.

'There's gypsies up on the field at the back o' the manse,' said Willie.

Hamish's eyes narrowed. 'An old bus?'

'Aye.'

'I'll come with you. They're not gypsies but travellers.'

'Commercial travellers, sir?'

'No, I'll tell you about them as we go along.'

Sure enough, there was the bus in the grassy field behind the manse.

Followed by Willie, Hamish knocked at the door. Cheryl opened it. 'Two pigs,' she said in disgust.

'Here now,' said Willie, 'there is no reason at all, at all to be using nasty words.'

'Go screw,' said Cheryl, and then, suddenly, she covered her face with her hands and began to sob pathetically, saying between her sobs, 'Why are you always persecuting me?'

'And just what do you think you are doing, Sergeant?' demanded a wrathful voice from behind Hamish. He swung round. Mrs Wellington, the minister's wife, stood there, and behind her was Sean, rocking lightly on his heels, a mocking look in his green eyes.

'I am moving these people on,' said Hamish.

'You have no right to do any such thing,' said Mrs Wellington wrathfully. 'I gave this young man permission to put his bus here, and that is all there is to it. These poor young people are hounded from pillar to post by bureaucratic monsters like yourself, Hamish Macbeth. These people of the road should be admired for their life-style.'

If you have given your permission,' said Hamish, 'then that is all right. But I shall be calling on you later.'

As he walked off with Willie, he heard behind him Sean's light, amused laugh. 'Get on to Strathbane,' said Hamish to Willie, 'and see if they have anything on their files on Sean Gourlay and Cheryl Higgins.'

'Herself was a bit dirty-mouthed,' said Willie, 'but he seemed nice enough.'

'He's as bad as she is and I have the feeling that he's dangerous.'

'Well, now, sir, I am in the way of being a student o' human nature,' said Willie. 'I took a corresponding course in the psychotry.'

'A correspondence course in psychiatry,' corrected Hamish, who always felt he was fighting a losing battle against Willie's mistakes and malapropisms.

'Didn't I just say that?' demanded Willie, aggrieved. 'Well, I would say from my experience that Sean Gourlay is just a regular, normal fellow.'

'Never mind. Check up on him anyway,' said Hamish. 'And by the way, we're invited up to the castle for dinner tonight by Miss Halburton-Smythe.'

'But we cannae dae that, sir,' said Willie patiently. 'That waud mean two of us off duty.'

'We leave a note on the door o' the police station to say where we are,' said Hamish, striving for patience. 'What's going to happen in Lochdubh? The same as all the nights since you've been here . . . nothing at all.'

'Well, I suppose . . .' Willie's voice trailed away and his mouth fell open. They had arrived outside the Italian restaurant and the beauty Hamish had seen earlier was down on her knees scrubbing the restaurant steps, her bottom waggling provocatively with each movement of the scrubbing brush. 'That's something you dinnae say these days,' said Willie, staring in admiration.

'What? A bum like that?' asked Hamish.

'No, a woman down on her knees scrubbing. I thought they were exstinked.'

'Nice day,' said Hamish loudly, raising his cap. The girl turned and looked up and then got to her feet, wiping her soapy hands on her apron.

'Just arrived?' pursued Hamish.

'Yes. Mr Ferrari send for me last month.'

'But you knew English already?'

'My mother, she is from Edinburgh. She go back to the village to get married. The village is outside Naples.'

She held out a small work-reddened hand. 'I am Sergeant Hamish Macbeth and this is PC Willie Lamont,' said Hamish, 'and you are . . .?'

'Lucia Livia.'

'And what do you think of Lochdubh, Miss Livia?'

'It is . . . very quiet,' she said, her eyes looking beyond them to the still loch.

A group of fishermen and forestry workers came along and stopped short, all of them staring at Lucia in silent admiration.

'I feel it is the duty o' the police tae look after newcomers to the village,' said Willie suddenly. 'Perhaps you waud allow me to show you around the place, Miss Livia?'

'I am not sure,' she said cautiously. 'I would have to ask Mr Ferrari. I work every evening.'

'Aye, well, just you ask him,' said Willie. 'You've left the corners o' the steps dirty. That'll no' do. Wait and I'll show ye.'

'For heffen's sake,' muttered Hamish, his Highland accent becoming more sibilant. But Willie was already down on his knees, scrubbing busily at the step.

'I'll say good day to you, Miss Livia,' said Hamish stiffly. 'Some of us haff the police work to do.'

Willie scrubbed on, unheeding.

Hamish walked gloomily back to the police station. In the small kitchen, everything gleamed and shone and the air smelled strongly of bleach and disinfectant. He made a cup of coffee and carried it through to the police station and sat down at the desk. He phoned Strathbane and spoke to Detective Jimmy Anderson, giving him the names of Cheryl and Sean. The address on Sean's driving licence had been a Glasgow one and Hamish remembered it clearly, Flat B, 189, Lombard Crescent. Anderson said he would check up on it and get back to him as soon as possible.

Hamish then went out again and along to the manse. The minister was alone in his study. 'Oh, Hamish,' he said, pushing away the sermon he had been working on, 'what brings you here?'

'It's those layabouts and their bus.'

'They are doing no harm, Hamish. The field is not used for anything. It's a small patch of weedy grass and nettles. Why shouldn't these young people have the use of it?'

'There's something about them I don't like. Besides, I'm surprised at you, Mr Wellington, for encouraging that kind of layabout.'

'Now, Hamish,' said the minister mildly, 'you know jobs are few and far between.'

'So why don't they go somewhere where there are jobs?' demanded Hamish, exasperated.

The minister chewed the end of his pencil in an abstracted way and then put it down. 'There is something appealing about their way of life,' he said. 'I sometimes think it would be wonderful to just take off and travel around without any responsibilities whatsoever.'

'And then who would pay the taxes?'

'They're both young,' said Mr Wellington comfortably. 'Time enough yet for them to grow up and become responsible.'

'Sean Gourlay is, I should guess, in his late twenties,' pointed out Hamish, 'and the girl has a gutter mouth.'

'Come now, she was charming to me.'

'Well, I feel you are being conned,' said Hamish. 'Don't say I didn't warn you!'

Hamish and Willie drove up to Tommel Castle Hotel that evening. Hamish climbed down from the Land Rover and sniffed the soft air with pleasure. The light evenings were back. Gone was the long dark tunnel of winter. A faint breeze blew in from the moors, scented with wild thyme. And then one of the castle cars, driven by a young woman, drove up and began to reverse to park next to the police Land Rover.

'Wait a minute,' shouted Willie, moving purposefully forward. 'You're no' doing it right. Hard left. Now straighten up! Straighten up. Dear God, lassie, how did you ever pass your test? Don't you know how to straighten up?'

Face scarlet with a mixture of fury and mortification, the woman parked at an angle and then climbed out and slammed the car door.

Willie shook his head. 'Women drivers,' he said. 'You'll need to do better than that.'

She gave him an angry look and walked off into the hotel without a word.

'Stop being Mr Know-All,' said Hamish. 'She'd probably haff done chust fine if you had left her alone. Now forget you're a cop, and try to be charming.'

Suddenly nervous, Willie tugged at his tie. 'Do I look all right, sir?'

'Yes, yes, just watch that mouth of yours.'

Priscilla met them in the entrance hall. 'Doris is waiting for us in the bar,' she said. 'I told her to get herself a drink and settle down. Some fool of a man was trying to tell her how to park.'

Hamish groaned inwardly. Doris Ward was a plain young woman with thick glasses and a rather rabbity mouth. She was wearing a blouse and skirt and a tartan waistcoat. She shook hands with Willie and Hamish and then said to Willie, 'I should have known you were a bobby.'

'Sorry about that,' said Willie awkwardly after a nudge in the ribs from Hamish's elbow. 'Forgot I was off duty.'

'I am sure you have more to do when you are *on* duty,' said Doris, 'than hector women drivers.'

'You're English, aren't you?' said Hamish, desperate to change the conversation. 'Thanks, Priscilla, I'll have any sort of soft drink, but Willie here will have a whisky.'

'Yes, I'm English,' said Doris. 'It's all very remote up here, isn't it?'

Everyone agreed that, yes, it was remote and then there was a heavy silence.

'Willie here is from the city, Strathbane,' said Hamish at last. 'He's finding it difficult to get used to village ways.'

'Do you have many friends in the village?' Doris asked Willie politely.

'No, not in Lochdubh,' said Willie, 'but I have a cliché of friends in Strathbane.'

'Clique,' moaned Hamish under his breath.

'Mind you,' said Willie, becoming expansive, 'I have always wanted to travel. I have an aunt in America I could go and see.'

'Which part of America?' asked Doris.

'She lives in a condom in San Francisco.'

Doris sniggered. 'Well, in these AIDS-ridden days, that's a very safe place to live.'

Willie looked at her, puzzled, and then his face cleared. 'Oh, aye, them condoms have secured cameras and guards and things like that.'

'Do you want to travel yourself, Doris?' asked Hamish.

'Oh, I don't know.' Behind her thick glasses, her eyes sent him a flirtatious look. 'I might settle for marriage.'

'Quite right too,' said Willie heartily. 'I must say, it is refreshing to meet the woman these days who disnae go in for all this fenimist rubbish.'

'You mean *feminist*,' corrected Doris. 'If you are going to criticize anything, at least pronounce it properly. Do you mean all women should settle for marriage and babies?'

'Why not?' demanded Willie, giving her a tolerant smile. 'That's what they're built for.'

'You're out of the Dark Ages,' said Priscilla smoothly. 'Dinner should be ready now. Carry your drinks through.'

'Get her to talk about herself,' hissed Hamish in Willie's ear as they walked towards the dining room.

But no sooner were they seated and waiting for the first course to be served than Doris selected a cigarette from a packet and lit up.

'Do you know you are ruining your lungs?' demanded Willie. 'That stuff's a killer and bad for the skin, too. I can already see it has –'

'What are we haffing for dinner?' said Hamish, his voice suddenly very loud and strained.

'Scotch broth to start,' said Priscilla, 'and then steak. We've got a new chef. We had to get rid of the old one,' she said to Doris, 'after that murder here, the one I told you about.'

Doris gazed at Hamish with admiration. 'I heard you'd solved it,' she said. 'Tell me all about it.'

Normally too shy to talk much about himself but frightened of Willie's gaffes, Hamish told her about it at length, but Priscilla saw to her irritation that Doris was entranced with Hamish and could hardly keep her eyes off him.

The evening went from bad to worse. Hamish had never before seen Willie drink anything stronger than tea or coffee. The whisky before dinner, the wine at dinner and the brandy afterwards went straight to his head. As soon as Hamish had finished talking, Willie began to talk about *his* cases, which sounded like a dismal catalogue of public harassment. He seemed a genius at finding out cars with bald tyres, cars with lapsed road tax, cars with various other faults, and every parking offence under the sun. He told what he obviously thought were hilarious stories of people who had become angry with him and what they had said. He laughed so hard, the tears ran down his face. Willie had never before enjoyed himself so much. He felt he was the life and soul of the party.

Hamish at last propelled a dreamily smiling Willie out to the Land Rover. 'You made a fine mess o' that, Willie,' he said as he drove down to Lochdubh through the heathery darkness. But there was no reply. Willie had fallen asleep.

What on earth am I going to do with him, thought Hamish wearily. Up on the field behind the manse, lights glowed behind the curtained windows of the bus. He did not like the sight. He did not like the feeling of this alien and dangerous presence in Lochdubh.

He then reassured himself with the thought that they would soon get bored and move on. The 'travellers' like to journey in convoys. It was odd to find two of them on their own.

He woke Willie outside the police station and ordered him sharply to go in and go to bed. Then he phoned Strathbane. Jimmy Anderson was working overtime and took the call. He had, he said, found nothing on Cheryl and Sean Gourlay from the Glasgow police except to confirm that Sean had taken his driving test in Glasgow recently, hence the new licence.

'Try Scotland Yard,' urged Hamish. 'See what they can come up with.'

'Whit? They're overworked down there as it is, complained Anderson. 'Whit's this Sean done?'

'Nothing . . . yet,' said Hamish. 'Look, just try them.'

'Try them yoursel',' said Anderson. 'We've got more than enough work here. In my opinion, you're going a bit ower the top about this Sean character. Wait till he does something.'

Hamish put down the receiver. He felt he had been a bit silly. There was no need to phone the Yard.

Besides, what could he have told Scotland

Yard anyway? That he had a bad feeling, an intuition?

Sean would be gone by next week at the latest. And with that comforting thought, Hamish went to bed.

Chapter Two

We believe no evil till the evil's done.
— Jean de la Fontaine

But a week later, the bus was still parked up behind the manse. A much cleaner and quieter Cheryl than Hamish had first met wandered about the village or up on the moors. She and Sean were hardly ever to be seen together. They seemed a popular enough pair with the villagers, who were all Highland enough to admire really genuine laziness when they saw it, and Hamish was irritated to overhear one of the village women saying, 'Thon Sean Gourlay can beat our Hamish any day when it comes to the idleness.'

Hamish felt this was particularly unfair, as he had suddenly been beset with a series of small accidents and crimes to deal with. There were frying-pan fires, minor car crashes, lost sheep, lost children, boundary disputes, poachers, and various other things which seemed like dramas at the outset and resolved themselves into minor happenings at the end. Particularly the three reported cases of lost children, who turned out to have been playing truant from school to go fishing. But it still meant a lot of paperwork, and Hamish found that easier to do himself than to spend hours correcting Willie's prose.

The weather was still unseasonably mild and all the burns and rivers were foaming with peaty water, like beer, as they rushed down from the hills and mountains fed by melting snow. The air was full of the sound of rushing water. Curlews piped on the moors, sailing over their nests, their long curved beaks giving them a prehistoric look. There were vast skies of milky blue and tremendous sunsets of feathery pink clouds, long bands of them, each cloud as delicate as a brush-stroke.

Hamish would have put Sean Gourlay out of his mind had he not found him hanging around the hotel gift shop where Priscilla worked.

Sean gave Hamish his usual mocking look as he strolled out of the shop. Hamish waited until he had gone and then said to Priscilla, 'You shouldn't encourage him.'

'Why not?' demanded Priscilla coolly. 'The first time he bought a silver-and-amethyst ring, and the second, a mohair shawl. He's a genuine customer, Hamish.'

24

'Where does he get the money?' demanded Hamish. 'I happen to know the pair o' them are drawing the dole from the post office.'

'Maybe he's got a private income,' said Priscilla. 'Look, Hamish, the way you go on and on about layabouts is a joke. You've never been a one for hard work yourself.'

'Aye, but I get my money honestly,' said Hamish, annoyed that she should defend Sean.

'Hamish, I happen to know that you poach salmon from the river.'

'Well, only the odd one.'

'Still, that's stealing. You're supposed to stop poaching.'

'It's the gangs that dynamite the rivers I'm after,' said Hamish huffily. 'I don't do any harm.'

'You must have less than ever to do now that you've got Willie,' pursued Priscilla.

'On the contrary, I've got double the work. That fellow *makes* work. That was a grand idea of yours to get him married off, but there isnae a woman in Lochdubh that would have him.'

'Seen anything of Doris?' asked Priscilla casually.

'She called at the police station a couple of times, just in a friendly way,' said Hamish defensively.

The phone on the wall rang shrilly and

Priscilla picked it up. 'It's for you,' she said, handing the receiver to Hamish.

Mrs Wellington's voice sounded shrill and harsh from the other end. 'Hamish, wee Roderick Fairley is trapped on a rock in the Anstey below the bridge and the river's rising by the minute. Where were you? Why isn't there anyone at the police station? Why –?'

Hamish dropped the receiver on the counter 'There's a wee boy stuck on a rock in the Anstey,' he said to Priscilla. 'See if you can get Willie.'

As he ran out, he could hear Mrs Wellington's voice still squawking from the receiver.

He drove fast down to the village. He could see a group of men and women hanging over the parapet of the hump-backed bridge over the River Anstey.

He jumped down from the Land Rover and pushed them aside.

Roderick Fairley, a chubby five-year-old with hair as flaming red as Hamish's own, was sitting astride a large rock in the middle of the river, which was foaming about him with a deafening roar.

'The river's rising every minute,' said a man at Hamish's ear. 'We'd throw the wee lad a rope but the force o' that water'd pull his arms frae their sockets.'

'Get a ladder,' said Hamish. He scrabbled down the side of the bridge and on to the riverbank. The force of the water was tremendous as it cascaded under the bridge and poured around large rocks like the one on which the child was sitting and then hurtled down the falls below. Rainbows rose in the air above the water. Hamish cupped his hands to call to the boy and then realized that Roderick would not be able to hear him above the force of the river.

'Here's Jimmy with the ladder,' came a voice, and Hamish twisted about. 'Bring it here,' he shouted, 'and we'll lay it from the bank to the rock.'

More faces peered over the parapet of the bridge. With the help of Jimmy Gordon, a forestry worker, Hamish laid the long ladder from the bank out to the rock. The terrified Roderick sat motionless, his mouth open in a soundless wail of fear.

'It's no' very steady,' shouted Jimmy.

Hamish asked, 'How did he get over there?'

'His friend says they was jumping frae rock tae rock and then the river rose sudden-like,' said Jimmy.

More men had come up. 'Now,' said Hamish, removing his cap and throwing it down on the bank, 'you lot hold the ladder steady.'

Hamish began to inch his way across. A great silence fell on the watching crowd. The roar of the water seemed to be louder and stronger. He pulled himself along the ladder, shouting as he did so, 'Don't be afraid, Roddy. I'm nearly there.'

And then the roar of the water became louder, and high above it rose a great keening wail of distress from the women on the bridge and on the banks. Hamish cast one frightened agonized look up the river and saw a wall of water rushing down the mountain towards the bridge and made a lunge and grabbed the child just as the water struck with full force.

Priscilla arrived just in time to see the crowd scatter from the bridge before the torrent struck, to see Hamish's red hair disappearing under the roaring flood. Stumbling and cursing and weeping, she made her way down towards the loch, over boulders and roots of shaggy fir trees, over tearing brambles and down to the beach. Her eyes raked the torrential stream and then the waters of the loch. Nothing.

From all over the village, people were running to the beach.

Priscilla stopped at the edge of the loch and stood panting. Mrs Fairley, the little boy's mother, was kneeling by the side of the water, crying out in Gaelic to the ancient gods to give her back her son.

And then the waters out in the loch broke and Hamish's head rose above them. He was holding the boy fast. He swam to shore while

Priscilla and the others waded out into the loch to meet him.

'Quick,' panted Hamish. 'He may be alive yet.'

The boy lay in his arms as still as death.

Hamish laid the boy face down on the beach and then began to pump his little arms up and down. Suddenly, water gushed from the boy's mouth and he set up a wail.

'He's alive. Roddy's alive.' The news spread out from the shoreline. Mrs Fairley fainted dead away. Dr Brodie arrived with his medical bag and gently pushed Hamish aside. Hamish sat down on the beach and put his head in his hands.

'Hamish, Hamish, I thought you were dead,' whispered Priscilla in his ear.

'Aye,' said Hamish on a sigh. 'I thought that myself.'

'Did you get a battering on the rocks?'

'No, there was such a lot of water, it swept us over them. Where did it all come from?'

'The Drum Loch at the top got filled up wi' melting snow and burst its banks,' said Archie Maclean, the fisherman. 'I hivnae seen the like since '46.'

An Air-Sea Rescue helicopter was landing a little way away along the beach. Hamish shivered. Dr Brodie said, 'He'll live. We'll get the helicopter to take him to hospital just to be sure. I'll attend to his mother and then she'd better go with him. You'd best go home and get a hot drink, Hamish. No broken bones?'

'No, I'm chust fine,' said Hamish. Followed by Priscilla, he made his way through the crowd. People slapped him on the back and shook his hand as he passed.

'Where's Willie?' asked Hamish.

'I don't know,' said Priscilla. 'I certainly didn't see him anywhere about.'

They had walked together along the beach away from the roaring, foaming river. They came to a flight of seaweedy stone steps cut into the sea-wall and climbed up them on to the waterfront. In front of them on the other side of the road was the Napoli restaurant, and there, at the side door of the restaurant, in the nonchalant manner of a stage-door Johnnie, was Willie.

'Willie!' shouted Hamish.

Willie started guiltily and then came running over, seemingly aware for the first time of the crowds, the helicopter and the dripping-wet Hamish. 'Whit happened?' he asked.

'Hamish has just rescued a little boy from drowning,' said Priscilla.

'And where were you?' demanded Hamish.

'I just called on that Miss Livia,' said Willie and then blushed. 'I wanted to see how she was getting on, it being part of my duties to look out for the welfare of the incomer.'

'Your job,' said Hamish wrathfully, 'is to look out for the welfare of people in trouble. Get back to the station and sit by that phone in the office until I tell you to move. Hop to it!'

Willie sulkily touched his cap with one forefinger and then slouched off.

'He'll haff to go,' said Hamish Macbeth.

The enterprising Mr Patel, who owned the local supermarket, had grabbed the shop video camera, which he rented out for occasions like weddings and dances, and had filmed the whole of Hamish Macbeth's dramatic rescue. He had then driven at great speed all the way to the headquarters of Highland Television, where he had sold them the video. Detective Chief Inspector Blair, on his day off, and planning to relax in front of the news, had all the doubtful pleasure of watching Hamish Macbeth on television. Mr Patel had done a good job. It was all there – from the striking of the wave and the disappearance of Hamish to his re-emergence in the loch. There was even a quote from Hamish. 'At his police station in Lochdubh, Sergeant Hamish Macbeth said he was only doing his job.' The quote had actually come from Willie, who had been told to say that to any of the press who phoned up.

Blair bit his thumb and scowled horribly at

the television set. Something would have to be done about Macbeth or he would go on getting promoted until he rose up the ranks and became his, Blair's, boss. There must be some way of discrediting Hamish.

The next day brought one of those abrupt changes in the weather in Sutherland. The wind moved round to the northeast and a blizzard whitened the countryside, blocking the roads and cutting Lochdubh off from the rest of the world.

Harry Tennant, the refuse collector, who was supposed to operate the gritting truck and snow-plough in bad weather, celebrating the prospect of overtime, fell asleep at the wheel and overturned the truck into a ditch, and so the roads remained ungritted and unsalted. Hamish felt Tommel Castle Hotel might have been moved to Australia, for all the chance he had of reaching it and seeing Priscilla. His near drowning had had a profound effect on him. He felt his life had hitherto been drifting amiably along, and somehow he felt he should now do something to alter it. He had not travelled. There was a whole world beyond Lochdubh, Lochdubh where he was snowed up in a police station with Willie and Towser for company. He had given away his television set as a bribe during his last big case, and so there was nothing to lighten the gloom, for he had read all of Mr Patel's small stock of paperbacks.

He went out into the driving snow to feed his hens and then shovelled a path to the gate, feeling as he did so that it was a sheer waste of time. The snow eased a little and as he looked along the waterfront, he could see a tall figure on skis heading out of the village. Sean. And Sean was surely going in the direction of Tommel Castle. He went back into the house and was strapping on his own skis to go in pursuit when Willie came through from the office. 'There's two climbers up on the mountain by the Drum Loch. They're trapped up on a crag. Thon shepherd, Jamie Macfarlane's jist phoned in tae say he can jist see them but cannae get tae them.'

'Have you phoned Mountain Rescue?'

'Not yet.'

'Do it and then get on your skis.'

'I havenae got any skis.'

'There's a spare pair out in the shed.'

'I cannae ski. There was nae need for sich activities in the town.'

'Get on the phone then.' Hamish stood up and strapped a pair of snow-shoes on his back and then slung a bag with an emergency medical kit over his shoulder.

Willie went rather sulkily back to the office.

Power's not a very good thing, thought Hamish ruefully, as he set out into the snow.

Willie's a pain in the neck, but I always seem to be snapping at him.

Priscilla had just finished stock-taking. As usual, she had opened the shop, despite the weather, because the hotel was full and guests often dropped in for a chat or to buy something to take home.

The door of the shop swung open, letting in a whirling cloud of snow. Sean Gourlay stood there, grinning, pulling off a ski mask.

'What brings you here?' asked Priscilla. 'It's hardly a day for shopping for souvenirs.'

He stooped down and took off his skis. Then he removed his anorak and swung it over the back of a chair. 'I thought I might get a cup of coffee and a chat,' he said, smiling at her. 'It's awfully boring with all this snow.'

He had come close to her as he spoke. He was, thought Priscilla, not for the first time, a devastatingly handsome man. But there was Cheryl.

'How's your girlfriend coping with it all?' she asked, backing away and then turning round to pour him a cup of coffee.

'Oh, whining as usual,' he said with a light laugh. He took the mug of coffee from her. 'Cheryl's not really my girlfriend, just a little creature who tags along.'

'Oh, really,' said Priscilla coolly.

'I know that sounds cruel, but she had been living with this chap and he threw her out, so she had nowhere else to go. What does a beauty like you find to do in Peasantville?'

'Helping to run a family hotel keeps me very busy,' said Priscilla. His very presence was making her feel claustrophobic. His grass-green eyes were glittering hypnotically and he was exuding a strong air of male virility.

'Never feel like running away from it all?'

'No. I like it here.'

'And what about boyfriends?'

'Mind your own business.'

He smiled at her, unruffled. 'Can't be much around here,' he said. 'You don't fit in. You're much too glamorous for a place like this.'

Priscilla gave an impatient little sigh. 'Do you want to buy anything?'

'I might.' His eyes roamed over the goods and then came to rest on Priscilla's coat and scarf, which were hanging on a hook behind the counter. 'Perhaps that scarf.'

'That's mine.'

'I'd like to buy it, nonetheless. I'd like something of yours.'

'Perhaps you had better go, Mr Gourlay.'

He came round the counter and stood next to her, very close. 'No, I don't think so,' he said softly. 'Not until I get that scarf.'

Priscilla backed off to the end of the counter and then she quickly pressed the alarm bell under it. Immediately she had done it, she felt silly. There was no need to feel so frightened of him. Men had made passes at her before.

'Finish your coffee and go,' she said firmly. 'You are wasting my time and I've got a job to do.'

The shop door crashed open and Dougie the gamekeeper stood there, a shotgun in his hand. 'I heard the bell,' he said.

Priscilla now felt thoroughly foolish. 'I must have pressed it by mistake. This is Mr Gourlay, Dougie. He's just leaving.'

Sean clipped on his skis and put on his coat. He pulled a black ski mask down over his face. ''Bye, beautiful,' he said. And then he was off.

'Did ye really press thon bell by accident?' asked Dougie.

'No,' said Priscilla. 'He scared me. I don't know why.'

'If he comes again,' said Dougie, 'jist ring the bell. And tell Hamish about this.'

'There's no need to tell Hamish,' said Priscilla. 'He's probably having a lovely time sitting in his kitchen with his feet on the stove.'

Then she gave an exclamation. 'My scarf's gone. He must have taken it.'

'Aye, weel, ye'll need tae phone Hamish now. That's theft.'

* * *

Sean skied easily down towards the village. He had heard gossip about the local bobby and Priscilla. Some said he was sweet on her, some said she was sweet on him. Whatever way, he planned to let Hamish see him wearing the scarf. Irritating that Highland pig would be a pleasure. And then he cursed under his breath. Who was to know whether Hamish would recognize that scarf? And what if that hoity-toity bitch called him to report a theft? Then Hamish would have him, Sean, just where he wanted him. Damn. He skied back and made his way across country so that he would arrive at the back of the shop. The snow was easing now. He looked in the window. Priscilla was just putting on her coat. Then she switched off the lights and went out and locked the shop door behind her.

He waited a few moments and then slid quietly round to the front. He unzipped a pocket in his anorak and took out a set of tools. He fiddled expertly with the lock until the tumblers clicked and then he eased the door open. It only took a moment to go quickly in and drop the scarf on the floor behind the counter. Then, just as quickly, he was outside again and had locked the door.

Hamish Macbeth had finally managed to reach the stranded climbers. One man was all right, the other man's leg had been broken in several places. Hamish gave him an injection and then sent up a distress flare, hoping he himself would not die of exposure before the Mountain Rescue team found them. He was too weary to give these inexperienced climbers a lecture on the folly of going up mountains in the north of Scotland in such weather. At least the snow was thinning slightly, but it was bitterly cold.

To his relief, he heard the whirring of helicopter blades and stood up and waved and shouted. One by one, they were hoisted into the helicopter, the injured man, strapped on to a stretcher, going first. 'Set me down in the village,' shouted Hamish above the roar of the engine and the pilot nodded.

How incredibly long it had taken to climb up the mountain to that crag and how quickly he was whizzed down and deposited on the waterfront in front of the wide car park of the deserted Lochdubh Hotel. He trudged wearily along to the police station, aching in every muscle.

He was furious to find the station unmanned and the kitchen stove out. But perhaps Willie had been called out on an emergency. He played back the answering service and heard Priscilla's voice asking him to call.

He sat down and phoned her at the hotel and listened to the tale of the theft of the scarf.

As he spoke to her, a churning, grating and whirring sound from outside told him that the Lochdubh snow-plough was once more back in action.

'Don't worry, Priscilla,' said Hamish. 'In a way that's the best news I've heard all day. I'll get rid of the bastard now.'

He left a note for Willie and then got out the Land Rover and moved off slowly along the newly cleared road. He stopped at the manse. The lights were on in the front room and he could clearly see Sean sitting at the dining table with the minister and his wife. There was no sign of Cheryl.

Well, he thought with satisfaction, what'll they think of their ewe lamb when they hear what I've got to say?

Mrs Wellington answered the door and looked with disfavour at the tall lanky figure of the sergeant.

'What is it, Hamish?'

'I want a word with Sean Gourlay.'

'Come in.'

Hamish followed her into the manse dining room. 'Sean Gourlay,' said Hamish, 'I am arresting you for theft and must ask you to accompany me to the police station. Anything you say –'

'Wait a minute,' said Sean easily. 'Theft of what?'

'Miss Halburton-Smythe's scarf. You took it from her gift shop this afternoon.'

'This is ridiculous,' exclaimed Mrs Wellington. 'She probably lost it.'

'It's an awful fuss to make about a scarf,' pointed out the minister. 'My umbrella was stolen last time I was in the Lochdubh bar, but no one did anything about that.'

'Nonetheless,' began Hamish, 'I –'

'Fiddlesticks!' said Mrs Wellington. 'We are going up right now to have a look at that gift shop, and mark my words, I am sure that scarf will be there. Young girls are so careless.'

'If you insist,' said Hamish. 'I can take a statement from Priscilla when I'm there.'

He drove them up to the castle and received a long lecture from Mrs Wellington about how police were always persecuting innocent citizens instead of going after real criminals.

Priscilla avoided looking at Sean as she led them all over to the gift shop and unlocked the door and switched on the lights. 'My scarf was with my coat on that hook behind the counter,' said Priscilla. 'Mr Gourlay said he wanted it.'

'Why?' asked Hamish sharply.

'It's a pretty one and I thought poor little Cheryl might like that.'

'That's not what you said to me,' protested Priscilla.

'This is all a fuss about nothing.' Mrs Wellington heaved her tweedy bulk behind the counter. 'You probably dropped that scarf. It's probably on the floor or somewhere. Why, here it is!' She held it up. 'Is this the scarf?'

'Yes,' said Priscilla, amazed. 'But how . . .?'

'How did it get there?' demanded Mrs Wellington. 'It didn't *get* anywhere. It just lay where you dropped it while you and this Highland layabout go around persecuting innocent young men. Oh, yes, Hamish, I know you've had your knife into poor Sean since the day he arrived.'

Her booming voice went remorselessly on and on while Hamish led them out to the car. She was still berating him when he dropped them off at the manse. 'And furthermore,' added Mrs Wellington, 'Miss Halburton-Smythe is being influenced by your tawdry mind. She is a lady. I know we are supposed to live in a classless society, but you would do better, Hamish Macbeth, to consort with your own kind of female!' Sean let out a chuckle of sheer delight.

Exhausted and furious, Hamish headed for home and then slammed on the brakes outside the Napoli restaurant. In the glow of candle-light he could see Willie seated at a window table.

He hurtled into the restaurant and towered over Willie, who cringed when he saw him.

'What the devil do you think you are doing?' howled Hamish.

41

Lucia rushed forward, her eyes full of tears. 'He was helping me,' she sobbed.

'Now then.' Old Mr Ferrari made his majestic way over. 'Haud yer wheest, Sergeant. The policeman here was helping Lucia clean the stove in the kitchen, and a grand job he made o' it, too. If all the coppers in Scotland were that helpful, the polis might hae a better image.'

Hamish sank down suddenly into the chair opposite Willie. 'Has everyone run mad?' he asked. 'Begin at the beginning, Willie, and tell me why you left your post.'

'It was awf'y quiet,' said Willie, 'and I thocht I'd jist call at the kitchen door to see if Lucia was all right. You see, I think it's part o' ma duties tae –'

'Yes, yes,' said Hamish. 'Skip that bit.'

'Well, herself was scrubbing at the stove wi' her wee hands and no' doin' the job well at all, at all. "You need pure ammonia for that," I says and I hae a bottle at the station. I only meant tae show her, but I got working and I didnae notice the time and then Mr Ferrari told me tae sit down and hae a glass o' wine. So I was jist having a glass o' chanter when you walked in.'

'Chianti,' said Hamish.

'Aye, weel, that's what I said.'

Hamish leaned back in his chair and surveyed his side-kick and took several deep breaths. If Willie had not been in Lochdubh, he thought, then his own day would have been much the same. Perhaps instead of constantly shouting at this infuriating policeman, it might be an idea to try some kindness.

'Some wine?' asked Mr Ferrari, deftly placing a glass in front of Hamish with one hand and holding up a bottle with the other.

Hamish Macbeth sighed. If you can't beat them, join them.

'Aye, that would be grand,' he said.

Chapter Three

'I'll hae the law on ye, ye randy! I'll hae yer life!'
— S. R. Crockett

A hard frost set in, turning Lochdubh into a Christmas card, and slowing the tumult of the River Anstey.

A subdued Willie told Hamish, when the sergeant had returned from an early-morning walk around the village, that headquarters at Strathbane had called and that he was to phone Superintendent Peter Daviot immediately.

Puzzled, Hamish phoned. The superintendent was not available but his secretary said the message was that he was to report to Strathbane in person as soon as possible, but she could not say what it was about.

'They're probably going to give you some sort o' medal,' said Willie, 'for the wee laddie's rescue.'

'Maybe,' said Hamish, fighting down a feeling of unease, 'although I thought if that was the case they might have sent me a formal letter. Keep the house warm, Willie, and I'll talk to that scunner Blair again about the central heating he promised me and didn't deliver. Check the sheep-dip papers and don't forget to cover the beat. The roads are terrible and someone could be in trouble. Use your own car. I'll need to take the Land Rover with me. I've forgotten to give the sheep their winter feed. Do that and make sure they've got water.'

'Hardly the job for a policeman,' mumbled Willie, who seemed determined to remain in a prolonged sulk.

No sooner had Hamish driven off than Willie darted into the office and phoned a friend at headquarters and asked why Hamish was being sent for.

'Oh, it's a right goings-on,' said the friend. 'Some tart's come in, screaming fur the super and carrying a baby. She says the bairn's father is Hamish Macbeth.'

'Oh, my!' exclaimed Willie in simple delight.

'He's goin' tae have that uniform and stripes ripped off him,' said the friend. 'I should think the police station at Lochdubh will be yours after today.'

Willie thanked him and put down the phone. He went through to the living quarters and looked slowly around. He could get that wallpaper with the nice Regency stripe for the living room and get rid of that nasty open fire which caused so much dust and put in one of those electric ones with the fake logs. He would take over Hamish's bedroom, which was larger than his own. He would rip the woodburning stove out of the kitchen and replace it with a Calor gas cooker. He rubbed his hands gleefully. And that battered armchair Hamish liked so much could go for a start. A good spring cleaning was what the place needed. Whistling cheerfully, he tied on an apron and got to work.

Hamish sat nervously in the superintendent's office in Strathbane Police Headquarters. Strathbane! How he hated the place. A dreary, soulless town on the edge of the sea, with rotting docks and rotten houses and a general grey air of failure.

Superintendent Peter Daviot came in and Hamish jumped to his feet.

'Sit down, Macbeth,' said the superintendent. No 'Hamish'. A bad sign.

'What's it about?' asked Hamish, wondering if Priscilla's father's water bailiff had seen him poaching on the river and reported him.

'It's about Maggie Dunlop.'

'Who?'

'Come, come, Sergeant, let's talk this out man to man. Maggie Dunlop is waiting downstairs with your son.'

'My –! This is a bad joke.'

'No, Macbeth, she has reliable witnesses and photographs to prove it.'

Hamish leaned back in his chair and said very quietly, 'Let's have the lassie in here. I'm fascinated.'

'Very well. I'm sorry about this. I thought you were doing so well, and the rescue of that little boy from the river was a credit to the force.' He pressed a bell on his desk and said, 'Send up Miss Dunlop. You will find her with Mr Blair.'

'Blair,' said Hamish slowly. 'Is he behind this?'

'I don't know what you mean. He happened to be here when she called – in great distress, I may add.'

After a few moments the door opened and Blair ushered in a scrawny girl clutching a dirty baby. 'Oh, Hamish,' she cried when she saw him. 'How could ye?'

'I've never seen you before in my life,' said Hamish flatly.

She began to weep and wail while the baby bawled. Blair thrust two photographs at Hamish. 'Whit hae ye tae say tae that, laddie?'

Hamish stared down at the photographs in bewilderment. They were two snapshots of him with Maggie. He was smiling and had an arm around her shoulders. In each photo he was in uniform. 'They must be fakes,' he said.

The baby abruptly stopped crying and looked at Hamish wide-eyed.

Mr Daviot leaned forward and clasped his hands. 'Now we all make mistakes. This happened three years ago, Miss Dunlop says. She says she's written to you several times begging for support money for the child, but you never answered.'

'And who is this reliable witness or witnesses?' demanded Hamish grimly.

'Mr and Mrs John Tullyfeather, who live next door to Maggie, can testify that you visited her frequently.'

'And where do they and this woman here live?'

'The Nelson Mandela block of flats down by the old dock. Stop this farce, Hamish. As you very well know, Miss Dunlop lives at number 23.'

Blair gave a coarse laugh. 'Ye cannae get yer leg over these days, Hamish, withoot paying the consequences.'

'That's quite enough of that,' snapped Mr Daviot. 'You may get back to your duties, Blair.'

Blair left reluctantly.

Hamish looked closely at the photographs again. He suddenly remembered the horrible time when the police station had been closed down in Lochdubh and he had been called to serve on the force in Strathbane. Before his blessed return to his village, where the locals had organized a crime wave to get him back, he had had his photograph taken down on the waterfront by Jimmy Anderson. But in those pictures he had been standing with his arm around WPC Pat Macleod. Jimmy had given him the film to get developed, but then Hamish had had the glad news of his return and had left the roll of film in his desk. So someone, probably Blair, had got the film and persuaded some bent photographer, probably himself – Hamish remembered the detective saying he had a darkroom at home – to fake up the photos.

'Could I haff a word with you in private, sir,' said Hamish.

'Indeed you can. This ugly business must be cleared up,' said Mr Daviot. 'Goodness, if the local press got their hands on this!' He rang the bell and told his secretary to take Miss Dunlop to the canteen and see that she had tea and cakes.

Maggie Dunlop left, strangely silent, but eyeing Hamish uneasily as she went.

Hamish tapped the photographs. 'If you ask Jimmy Anderson, he will remember taking photos of me with Policewoman Macleod in that location. Someone has found the film, taken photos of this Maggie and faked them.'

'Who would do such a thing?'

'Someone who didn't like me being made sergeant or getting all that coverage on television?'

'If you mean a jealous member of the police force, you must be mistaken! You may as well tell the truth.'

'Furthermore, sir,' said Hamish quietly, 'did you check whether this Maggie Dunlop and the reliable witnesses have criminal backgrounds?'

'Of course not. Why?'

'Chust do me a favour,' said Hamish, 'and ask. My job's on the line.'

'Oh, very well.' Mr Daviot picked up the phone and rapped the necessary instructions down it. Hamish leaned back in his chair and folded his arms. 'We'll chust wait and see.'

It seemed an age before the phone rang. Mr Daviot snatched it up and listened intently. Then he gazed at Hamish as the voice went on, his eyes round.

He finally put the phone down and said awkwardly, 'Well, Hamish, it seems as if you have the right of it. I asked Pat Macleod to check and there was nothing on our files against either of them, but she's a bright girl and she checked the Central Scottish Criminal Records by phone. Maggie Dunlop, or certainly a Maggie Dunlop who fits the description of your accuser, was a well-known prostitute in Glasgow. She became pregnant and decided to start a new life up here. James Tullyfeather is also from Glasgow and has just finished doing ten years for armed robbery. There can't be more than one robber with a name like Tullyfeather. This is terrible. Who would do such a thing to you? Wait here.' He shot out of the door.

So, thought Hamish, beginning to relax. Blair's up to his tricks. If Maggie Dunlop's still in the canteen, I'm a Dutchman. Blair would be hanging about to find out what was going on and he'd know Pat was checking up. He must nearly have had a heart attack when she moved over to checking the Central Criminal Records.

After a long time, the superintendent came back and slumped down heavily into his chair. 'What a mess,' he said. 'Maggie Dunlop has disappeared. I went myself in a squad car round to Nelson Mandela House but the flat was empty, and the Tullyfeathers had gone as well. Someone in this station must be responsible. Perhaps it was meant as a joke?'

'Taking a joke a bit far when it meant faking those photographs,' pointed out Hamish, who was beginning to enjoy himself.

'Dear me, yes. There will be a full investigation. Have you yourself any idea who ...? What about that policewoman, Mary Graham, who had some sort of spite against you?'

'Oh, I shouldn't think it was her,' said

Hamish blithely. 'This has upset me a lot, sir. Do you mind if I go home?'

'By all means. You are taking this remarkably well, Hamish. If there is anything I can do for you, anything at all . . .'

Willie, thought Hamish, but not yet.

He said goodbye and ambled down the stairs and into the detectives' room and looked around. There was no sign of Blair. He was not surprised. He went out and had a meal and then returned to the detectives' room. This time, Blair was sitting at his desk.

'Oh, aye, Hamish,' he said with false heartiness. 'Glad ye got that wee problem sorted out.'

Hamish pulled up a chair close to Blair and leaned forward. 'Don't ever do that again,' he whispered, 'and unless you get me the central heating for my police station, I'll track down that brass nail you coerced into lying and I'll have *you* out of a job.'

'I don't know whit you're talking about,' muttered Blair.

'Do I get the central heating or not?'

'Aye, of course, Hamish. I promised, didn't I? Mind you, Daviot's cutting down on regional expenses and –'

'You've got a week,' said Hamish and rose and left.

Blair watched him go and then lumbered to his feet. He caught Mr Daviot just as the superintendent was leaving.

'I saw Macbeth,' said Blair. 'He's in a fair taking over the way he's been treated.'

'Oh, dear,' said Mr Daviot. 'He seemed so good about it all. Of course I did tell him if there was anything we could do for him to let us know.'

'As tae that, I meant to tell you, sir, that he's been wanting the central heating for that bit o' a polis station in Lochdubh.'

'Then arrange it! Arrange it right away!'

'Yes, sir. Right away, sir. How's the lady wife, sir?'

'Tolerably well, thank you. She was delighted with the flowers you sent her.'

'Only too happy tae please, sir, you know that.'

Blair followed the superintendent down the stairs, oiling and complimenting. Superintendent Daviot saw nothing wrong with this. In fact, he enjoyed it immensely.

Blair finally got back to his desk. What had come over him to try that trick on Hamish? He had been so pleased with the job he'd done on those photographs. Now he'd had to pay Maggie and the Tullyfeathers to run for it – pay them a lot. It must have been the drink. He would never drink again. Well, maybe just the one to steady his nerves. He slid open the bottom drawer of his desk and eased the bottle out.

* * *

54

Hamish drove slowly and carefully back to Lochdubh. It was so cold that even the salty slush on the roads was beginning to freeze hard.

A small cold moon was shining down on the snow-covered moors. He braked hard as a stag skittered across the road in front of him. He drove on through the moon landscape until he topped the rise of the road which led down to Lochdubh. Bright stars were burning above and shining in the still waters of the loch below. Home, he thought, home and comfort. A glass of whisky, light the fire, relax.

But when he pulled up at the police station it was to see the kitchen door and front door standing open and piles of furniture in the small drive at the side. From the inside came the busy sound of vacuuming.

He edged his way around the furniture and walked in. Willie was through in the living room. He was pushing the vacuum around the carpet and whistling cheerfully.

'Willie!' roared Hamish, bending down and whipping the vacuum cord so that the plug shot out of the wall.

Willie turned slowly and stared at Hamish in ludicrous dismay. 'It's yerself.'

'What the hell are you doing to my home?' demanded Hamish.

'I thought I waud give it a wee bittie o' a spring clean,' said Willie miserably.

'Get this straight,' said Hamish. 'You occupy one bedroom. The rest is mine – my furniture, my books, my carpet, my kitchen ... mine, mine, mine. Put everything back the way it was, close the doors, heat the place up. You've got one hour to do it. And don't ever let me see you do any housekeeping here again.'

Hamish turned and strode out. Willie blinked and looked slowly about at the ruin of his dream. Gone forever, oh lovely Regency-striped paper. Gone forever, synthetic dust-free log fire.

Hamish drove to Tommel Castle Hotel, parked and went in search of Priscilla.

She was in the hotel office, sitting in front of a computer. 'Working late,' commented Hamish.

'Yes, Mr Johnson's got a bad cold.' Mr Johnson was the manager. 'Sit down, Hamish. You don't look your usual relaxed self. What's up?'

He told her all about Blair's perfidy. 'So,' she said when he had finished, 'that'll leave a gap in the ranks.'

'How come?'

'Well, Blair'll be out on his ear.'

'No, he won't. I didn't tell Daviot I knew it was Blair.'

'Why not?'

'I told Blair to get the central heating put in instead.'

'Hamish Macbeth, no detective should be

56

allowed to stay in the force after pulling a trick like that. Forget about the central heating. Get on to the phone now and tell Daviot you know it was Blair.'

'No point in that,' said Hamish uneasily. 'He'll have destroyed any evidence in his darkroom, and that precious pair he got to bear false witness will be long gone.'

'They can be found,' snapped Priscilla. 'You know that.'

Hamish looked at her in irritation. 'Look, Blair's had it in for me for a long time. I can cope. He's not bent when it comes to the general public. In fact, he's quite a good policeman in his plodding way.'

'When he's not coercing one ex-prostitute and one ex-burglar to lie for him to get you out of a job!'

'Priscilla, let it go. It's my business, not yours.'

She eyed him coldly. 'You're a born moocher. When it comes to getting something for nothing, then you'd turn a blind eye to murder.'

'That iss going too far!'

They both stared at each other in dislike. Hamish seized his cap, which he had placed on her desk when he arrived, noticing that the brim was cracked, for it was his second-best one, his good one having been lost in the river when he rescued the boy. 'I haff nothing mair tae say tae ye,' said Hamish, stalking out and spoiling the effect by knocking into an umbrella stand at the door and sending the contents flying. He picked up the assortment of walking-sticks and umbrellas and shoved them back into the uprighted stand.

Outside, he got into the car. He did not want to go straight back to the police station. He decided to call on Dr Brodie and his wife, Angela.

The doctor welcomed him, saying Angela was off at Stirling University on some course to do with her Open University degree. Hamish told him the tale of Blair and the doctor laughed appreciatively. 'So you'll be getting the central heating at last. How's that wee moron of yours getting on?'

Correctly identifying the moron as Willie, Hamish told him of the spring cleaning of the police station. 'That's bad,' said Dr Brodie, shaking his head. He handed Hamish a glass of whisky and then shovelled two dogs off the sofa so that Hamish could find a place to sit down. 'Remember when Angela had that spell of frantic cleaning? Man, it was terrible. Each house should have a little of its own family dirt. Gives the place character. I see you've still got your beatniks up at the back of the manse.'

'They don't call them beatniks any more,' said Hamish gloomily, still thinking of Priscilla's angry face. 'They call themselves the travellers or new travellers and try to claim the same rights as the gypsies. That pair has me fair puzzled. You see, normally these travellers like to go around in convoys, making some landowner's life hell. Landowner screams for the police, complains his land is being turned into a sewer, that the travellers' children aren't going to school and that drugs are traded openly. If he has enough power, then the police come in to move them on. Press arrive in droves. Next day letters in the papers from Church of England vicars and so on, complaining about harassing these poor innocent people, and the landowner is nothing but a bloated capitalist. A few people complain that the travellers are allowed to run around without road taxes and on bald wheels and all the other crimes for which John Smith is regularly stopped by the police and hauled over the coals, and then by the following day it's all forgotten until the travellers cause the next batch of trouble and then it all starts up again. But this pair have admittedly an old bus, but the tax is paid and he's got a clean licence and the tyres are good. What are they after?'

'Maybe not after anything,' said Dr Brodie, throwing another lump of peat on the ash-choked fire. 'Maybe genuine drifters.'

'Then there was Priscilla's scarf. She said he'd taken it. Mrs Wellington says she's probably dropped it behind the counter, and sure enough, there it is.'

'Priscilla doesn't make mistakes,' said Dr Brodie.

'No, she's barely human, and that's a fact,' complained Hamish.

Dr Brodie gave him a quizzical look, waiting for more, but instead Hamish said, 'If only I could get some lassie to fancy Willie and take him off my hands.'

'There's another way you could go about it,' said the doctor slyly.

'Aye, what's that?'

'Get married yourself.'

'There's nobody I fancy.'

'Except Priscilla. Forget Priscilla. Do you know Priscilla? I've known her since she was a wee lassie and I don't really know her. Very self-contained. She'll eventually marry the right bloke, some landowner, and we'll never know whether it was love or whether she was doing the right thing to please her parents. What about that new luscious lovely at the restaurant?'

'Lucia? Oh, everyone's after her, including Willie, and Willie hasn't a hope in hell. I gather his idea of courtship is telling her how to scrub the steps and clean the cooker.'

'There's Maisie Gowan.'

'Maisie Gowan's eighteen years old!'

'What's up wi' that? She fancies you. Then there's that Doris Ward from the hotel.'

'No, not her,' said Hamish. 'I don't want anyone. I want my old life back. I want rid of Willie. Man, this power is the terrible thing. When I had no one to boss but myself, I was that easygoing. Now I breathe down Willie's neck and snap if he doesn't haff the paperwork chust the way it should be. Ach, the man's a fair scunner, but I make things worse.'

'Never mind. Have another whisky,' said the doctor. 'It's this bitter weather. Very claustrophobic. The good weather'll be along soon and everything will be more open and relaxed.'

'Is there anything on the telly?' asked Hamish, looking longingly at the set in the corner. 'Willie had one but he got rid of it because he says he doesn't believe in it, chust as if it wass a type of religion.'

'Wait and I'll look up the paper and see what's on,' said the doctor, judging by the hissing sibilancy of Hamish's Highland accent that he was really upset. 'Here we are, BBC 1: "Whither England? Mary Pipps of the former Communist Party discusses plans for a European future." Dear me. BBC 2: "The rape of the Brazilian rain forests." Not again. You know what's caused the demise of the Brazilian rain forests, Hamish? Camera crews trudging all over the place. Grampian: "The Reverend Mackintosh of Strathbane Free Presbyterian Church gives his view on the spread of AIDS in Africa." Nothing left but Channel 4, let me see

. . . ah, "Highlights of the Gulf War", a repeat of last year's showing. Well, Hamish?'

'None of that. Can I take a look through your paperbacks and borrow a hot-water bottle? Willie threw my hot-water bottle out. He said the rubber was perished.'

'You sound like a man with a nagging wife. The books are over there; help yourself.'

Hamish, after much deliberation, chose an American detective story of the tough-cop variety. He collected a hot-water bottle and then crunched his way out through the icy snow on the doctor's unswept garden path. Great stars still burnt overhead but were beginning to be covered with thin high trails of cloud. He sniffed the air. A change was coming. The air smelt damp, rain-damp, not the metallic smell of snow.

He drove slowly to the police station. The furniture was gone from outside. Inside, the stove was blazing merrily in the kitchen. Everything smelt damply of ammonia and disinfectant. He took a look around the rest of the place. Willie's bedroom door was tightly shut, a mute reproach to Hamish's lack of understanding about housekeeping. Hamish went back to the kitchen and sat in front of the fire and opened the detective story. In it, the detective had a blonde girlfriend whom he treated abominably, something which seemed to make her even more adoring. Long and careful questioning of suspects was out of the question. He simply slapped them around until he got the answers. It was as remote a way of life to Hamish as an Arthurian legend. He read happily and finally went to bed with much of his old good-natured frame of mind restored. Let Willie clean and scrub and write reports in convoluted English. If he just ignored the man and went about his own ways, then life would be tolerable. As for Priscilla . . .?

Pompous hard-faced bitch, he thought, clutching the comforting hot-water bottle to his stomach. Who needs her anyway?

The weather again went in for one of its abrupt changes and heralded in the morning light with a blast of wind which roared into the loch and departed at the other end with an eldritch screech. Following it came the rain, steady, drenching rain. Once more the River Anstey was in tumult and the bridge was being seriously damaged by the pressure of the roaring flood. The village council met to decide whether to opt for a completely new bridge by the side of the old one, a new one which could take two lanes of traffic. But the die-hards wanted the old bridge. It was picturesque and one of the much photographed sights of the village.

Willie, sensing there was some sort of a truce, kept his housekeeping to a minimum, but when Hamish made no protest, he was soon happily back, polishing everything in sight.

But his happiness was dimmed by the fact that Lucia was walking out with Jimmy Gordon, the forestry worker. Jimmy was tall and fairly good-looking. Everyone in the village said they made a handsome couple.

Hamish had elected to do the outer reaches of the beat by car, leaving Willie to cover the village beat on foot. Somehow, wherever Jimmy walked with Lucia, Willie was never far behind.

'Would ye no' like tae come for a bit o' a drive up in the hills wi' me?' Jimmy was asking Lucia. 'We cannae get away from the polis.'

Lucia shook her head. Mr Ferrari said she was allowed to go for walks with Jimmy in the village and always where they could be seen. She glanced back at Willie and then said in her soft voice and very slowly, for she was always translating what she said in her mind from Italian to English, 'What is your idea of marriage, Jeemy?'

He took her hand in his. 'I want a wee wife to work and clean fur me, someone pretty tae come home tae in the evenings.'

'Would you wish me to iron your shirts?'

'Aye, that would be grand. Look at this one. It's a' crumpled.'

'Why don't you iron it yourself, Jeemy?'

He gave a great laugh and then flung an arm about her shoulders. 'That's women's work.'

Lucia gently disengaged herself.

Jimmy never knew what he had said wrong. But after that when he called at the kitchen door for Lucia, it was always old Mr Ferrari who answered and who told him that Lucia was too busy to see him.

Chapter Four

They flee from me, that sometime did me seek.
— Sir Thomas Wyatt

The good weather did not come all at once. At first there was a lessening of the wind, then the rain decreased to a thin drizzle and soon the rain ceased altogether, letting fitful rays of watery sunlight through the clouds. The days grew perceptibly warmer until even Hamish Macbeth, who delighted in his new central heating, was forced to admit that the police station was becoming like a hothouse. And then one day all the clouds rolled back and pale-blue skies stretched above Lochdubh, and the River Anstey at long last settled back down into its familiar banks, leaving a path of torn trees and bleached grass on either side as a record of its recent fury.

But the coming of the idyllic weather made Hamish Macbeth realize that he was becoming oddly unpopular. Angela Brodie, the doctor's wife, went out of her way to avoid him, as did Mrs Wellington. No more did Priscilla drop in on him for a chat. Even Nessie and Jessie Currie, the village spinster sisters, dived indoors and left their gardening tools scattered on the lawn when they saw him coming.

And for some reason, Hamish felt it all had something to do with Sean Gourlay. The bus was still there, looking to Hamish like a cancerous sore in the heart of the village. But he could not ask Sean to move on because of a feeling of evil, or rather a premonition of evil to come. He knew several of the villagers, the Misses Curries and Angela among them, had been visitors to the bus. Cheryl was occasionally to be seen about the village, much cleaned up and quiet, always on her own and talking to no one. Hamish was sure Sean had started some campaign to turn the villagers against him.

And then there was the strange behaviour of Mr Wellington, the minister. Like most churches these days, Mr Wellington's was sparsely attended, although the organizations connected with the church were as busy as ever. Most women in the village belonged to the Mothers' Union, of which Mrs Wellington was the chairwoman. The Boy Scouts and Girl Guides were both well attended. But gradually the church began to fill up on Sundays and Hamish was surprised to see members of the Free Presbyterian Church, members from the Free Church of Scotland, and from the Unitarians all neglecting their own kirks to go and hear Mr Wellington preach. What could be the reason? Hamish decided to find out. He told Willie to man the phone in the police office and went along to the church himself, meeting the fisherman, Archie Maclean, and his wife on the way.

'I've never known you to go to the kirk before,' said Hamish.

'Aye, but this is different,' said Archie. 'Mr Wellington preaches a rare sermon. We've heard naethin' like it since the auld days.'

Hamish was intrigued. On his rare visits to church, he had tried to keep awake as Mr Wellington's gentle scholarly voice wrestled with one of the more esoteric points of the Bible. Hamish often thought it sounded as if the minister were reasoning with himself.

He slid into a pew at the back.

The hymns were of the variety now frowned upon by liberal churchmen of all denominations as being too militant: 'Stand Up, Stand Up for Jesus, Ye Soldiers of the Lord', and 'Onward, Christian Soldiers'.

Then the minister climbed up into the high pulpit and looked down at a sheaf of yellowing notes. Hamish was surprised. Before, the minister's sermons had been extempore, or rather so well rehearsed that he spoke without notes.

Then he suddenly looked down at his flock and said in a harsh voice Hamish had never heard him use before, 'There are many of you here who will all burn in hell!'

There was a pleasurable indrawing of breath. Mrs Maclean edged a peppermint into her mouth. For some reason it was considered all right to eat peppermints in church, although chocolates would be considered downright sinful.

'Yes,' went on the minister, 'there are many of you who are liars and fornicators, and your lot will be to be cast into the pit where your flesh will fry, yea, and your crackling skin will be pricked with pitchforks by demons.'

The sermon ranted on for one hour and forty minutes. Hamish sat stunned. It was only when the minister summed up by asking them all to pray to God to protect them from the evil that was Napoleon Bonaparte that a glimmer of understanding began to dawn in his hazel eyes.

Curious and beginning to be half-worried, half-amused, he also went to the evening service. He was late and had to stand at the back, for the church was full to overflowing.

He was among the last to leave. He shook Mr Wellington's hand and said quietly, 'Can I drop up to the manse and have a word with you?'

'Yes, Hamish,' said the minister absent-mindedly. 'I shall be there to hear your troubles.'

'It's your troubles I'm thinking about,' said Hamish, but the minister was already shaking hands with a couple behind him and receiving their plaudits.

Hamish went up to the manse later, glad to find the minister on his own.

'What can I do for you?' asked Mr Wellington.

'What's come over you?' asked Hamish. 'You never were a one for all that fire and brimstone.'

'It brings people to church and instills a fear of God in them which is what I am here for,' said the minister primly.

'But it's not like you,' expostulated Hamish. 'You know what I think? I think that one day you couldn't think of a sermon and so you found some old ones and used one of them instead. Instant success! So you went on doing it. You're a walking horror movie. You'll have the children terrified to go to sleep at night. You don't even listen to what you're saying, which is why you left in the bit about Napoleon.'

The minister flushed angrily and glared at the wall.

'Come on, what's been happening?' asked Hamish gently.

Mr Wellington clasped his hands and swung to face Hamish. 'I've lost my faith,' he said. 'No words of mine have any meaning any more. In despair, yes, I used old sermons I found in a box in the attic. It's what they want. It brings them to the kirk.'

'Aye, so would a strip-tease. Surely you've lost your faith afore? It happens from time to time.'

'No, never.'

Hamish leaned back in his chair and clasped his hands behind his head. 'Has this anything to do with Sean Gourlay?'

'He did question me,' said the minister awkwardly. 'People here do not question ministers, and maybe they should. We get complacent, arrogant. He showed me pictures of refugees stumbling along roads pitted with bomb craters, of thousands dying after floods and tornadoes, and he asked me seriously how I could believe in a God of love.'

'But you can't defend the indefensible,' said Hamish wearily. 'Blind faith's the only answer, you know that. You must have had all thae arguments dinned in your ears when you were a student.'

'I am out of the world up here, Hamish. As Sean rightly pointed out, I have an easy life while millions are starving and suffering under the lash of the God I worship.'

'There are millions who would suffer a

damn sight more if they didnae have something tae believe in,' said Hamish angrily. 'How dae ye think they would feel if they were told that this is it, this is all there is, and after the grave, there is nothing?'

'My wife feels the same as I do,' he said heavily. 'It has affected her badly. She is a shadow of her former self.'

Spiritually but not physically, thought Hamish, who had seen the large tweedy bulk of Mrs Wellington in church that evening. 'Don't make any rash decisions,' said Hamish. 'Give it a few months. Talk to some other members of the clergy. Father Peter along at the Roman Catholic church seems a good man, and a clever one, too. Have a word with him.'

The minister smiled wryly. 'I do not know what my flock would think if they saw me consulting a Roman Catholic.'

'We're all ecumenical these days,' pointed out Hamish. 'Anyway, no one need know. Run along and see him. It's all the one God.'

When Hamish left, he strolled along the waterfront wondering if he himself believed anything he had said, wondering if there really was anything far beyond the first stars which were beginning to glitter in a pale-green sky.

With a sigh he went into the police station, to be met with a delicious smell. 'You're late for dinner,' said Willie, sliding a plate of beef casserole, which smelt of rich wine sauce, on to the table.

'Where did this come from?' asked Hamish.

'Mr Ferrari,' said Willie, deftly opening a bottle of Italian wine.

He's been cleaning the restaurant stove again, thought Hamish, but was too grateful for the delicious meal to say so.

After dinner, the phone rang. It was Jimmy Anderson from Strathbane. 'I took pity on ye, Hamish,' said the detective, 'and contacted the Yard. Sean Gourlay's got a record.'

'Tell me about it,' said Hamish eagerly.

'Nothing great, mind you, petty larceny, possession of cannabis, disturbance of the peace. Nothing for the last three years. Was in Hong Kong, where he got his first driving licence. Let it lapse and took the test in Glasgow.'

'Well, send me up a report,' said Hamish. 'It might do to get him off the manse field and out of this village.'

Willie came into the police office. 'The doctor's here tae see you,' he said.

Hamish rang off and turned to face an agitated Dr Brodie. 'I was making an inventory of the drugs cabinet, Hamish, and there's four packets of morphine missing.'

'I'd better come down and have a look at the cabinet. I cannae remember. Is it easy tae get into?' asked Hamish.

'No, it's padlocked and it's got a metal grille over it.'

'And nothing's been broken?'

'Not that I can see.'

Hamish dialled Strathbane and reported the theft, asking for a forensic team to be sent up in the morning. 'And while you're at it,' he said, 'get me a search warrant for Sean Gourlay's bus.'

'What, the traveller?' exclaimed the doctor. 'But he hasn't been near the surgery.'

'Well, we'll see,' said Hamish. 'Come on, Willie. Let's go and have a look.' They followed the doctor to his home.

Angela, the doctor's wife, gave Hamish a nervous look. 'Isn't it terrible?' she gasped.

'We'll see if we can find any clues,' said Hamish. Dr Brodie collected the keys to the surgery, which was along the road from his home.

Hamish examined the locks of the surgery carefully and then, inside, inspected the cabinet. 'When do you think the packets of morphine were taken?' he asked.

'That's the devil of it,' said Dr Brodie. 'I haven't really checked anything for six months. This is all I need.'

'Well, we'd best lock everything up again and let no one near it until after the forensic team's arrived,' said Hamish.

Hamish fully expected Detective Chief Inspector Blair to arrive on the following morning, but it was an Inspector Turnbull, a dour Aberdonian who arrived with Detective Jimmy Anderson and three uniformed policemen as well as the forensic team. He had a search warrant for Sean's bus and listened carefully as Hamish described Sean's criminal record.

Sean and Cheryl were brought down to the police station, where they were both searched, and then Sean was asked to take them to the bus.

Sean opened the door for them and then examined the search warrant again carefully. 'If you and your lady will just step outside,' said Inspector Turnbull, 'we'll be as quick as we can.'

The day was fine and mild. Sean and Cheryl sat side by side on a large packing case on the grass. Hamish noticed that they did not speak to each other.

He found himself praying to the God he was not quite sure he believed in for drugs to be found. He felt Sean was an evil influence on the village and wanted him out of it.

At long last, Turnbull emerged. 'Nothing,' he said to Hamish.

'Great stinking pigs,' muttered Cheryl, but Sean put a hand on her arm and remarked pleasantly, 'You really must stop harassing us,

Inspector, just because we don't fit into any conventional pattern.'

'Oh, I wouldnae say that,' said Turnbull. 'There's a lot o' you long-haired layabouts crawling about Scotland.'

'My hair is not long, and if you don't watch your mouth, Inspector, I shall sue you for harassment. You've found nothing, so shove off.'

Hamish suddenly said, 'Better check under the bus, Inspector, just in case.'

He had the satisfaction of seeing a look of alarm on Cheryl's face.

Sean lit a cigarette and eyed Hamish through the smoke. 'Determined to find me guilty, eh? I think it's time I phoned the press.'

He loped off in the direction of the manse. Hamish watched while the Calor gas tank outside the bus was unhitched, as were the cables from the bus to the manse, Sean obviously leeching electricity supplies from the minister. The keys, as Cheryl informed them, were in the blank, blank, blanking ignition. The bus roared into life and moved forward.

To Hamish's delight, there were loose sods of earth under the bus which, when lifted, revealed a hole about three feet square, recently dug. But it turned out to be full of rubbish – Coke cans, bottles and scraps of paper.

Whatever had been hidden there, and Hamish was sure something had been hidden there, had gone. But who could have alerted Sean? Willie was a gossip, but Willie had been close to him, Hamish, since the doctor had first reported the theft.

Cheryl put up an arm to brush her hair out of her eyes. Her loose sleeve rolled back. Hamish saw ugly bruises on her thin arm.

But there was nothing he could do about that unless Cheryl showed any signs of wanting to report Sean for beating her up, and from the way she had suddenly started to scream obscenities at the police, it was highly doubtful if she ever would. But what did Mrs Wellington think when she heard the girl running off at the mouth like that? Possibly she hadn't heard her. Possibly Cheryl reserved her swear-words for the police.

Next day the *Strathbane and Highland Gazette* carried a photograph of Sean and Cheryl on the front page. Sean was looking like a film star and Cheryl was attired in a pretty flowered cotton dress, with her hair done in two pigtails. The article quoted Sean as saying that they were a couple who only wanted to be left alone to enjoy the beautiful Highlands of Scotland but that they were being persecuted by the police. Inspector Turnbull was correctly quoted, describing Sean as a long-haired layabout. The article finished by saying that the couple were living in a converted bus on manse land with the full approval of the minister and his wife.

So that was that, apart from a stern warning from Strathbane not to go near the couple again unless evidence was concrete.

Sean and Cheryl had purchased from somewhere a small motor scooter, and one day, they roared off on it. But their bus still stood up on the manse field. Hamish, however, was glad to see them go, and hoped they would stay away for a few days at least.

But while they were gone, Hamish received an agitated caller, the treasurer of the Mothers' Union, Mrs Battersby. She was a thin, pale woman in her mid-forties with thick glasses, wispy hair and dressed in a wool two-piece she had knitted herself out of one of Patel's 'special offers', a sulphurous-yellow yarn. 'There's one hundred pounds missing from the kitty,' she said.

Hamish's thoughts immediately flew to Sean. 'When do you think it was taken?' he asked.

'Let me see, I counted it on Sunday, for Mrs Anderson had given me ten pounds. We have been collecting for Famine Relief. Then this morning, Mrs Gunn gave me five pounds and I opened up the box to add that money to it and thought I'd better just count it all over again and log it in the book and I immediately saw that one hundred pounds had gone!'

Hamish's heart sank. Sean and Cheryl had left last Saturday. They couldn't have taken it.

'How much was there altogether?' he asked.

'One hundred and forty-five pounds and twenty-three pee.'

'It's a wonder the lot wasn't taken.'

'Ah, you see, the hundred was in notes and the remainder is just in small change.'

'I'd better come along and hae a look,' said Hamish. 'Willie, you come as well.'

Willie, who had come through from the kitchen, began to remove his apron. 'Aye, thon's the grand lad you have there,' said Mrs Battersby despite her distress at the theft. 'Always cleaning.'

Hamish, in order to keep relations with Willie as easy as possible, had allowed the policeman to continue housekeeping. It seemed to be Willie's only interest in life. A new cleaner on the market was judged by Willie with all the care of a connoisseur sampling a rare wine. It was a pity, thought Hamish, that he had under him a policeman who showed so little interest in policing.

They walked together towards the church hall. 'So the funds are kept here,' said Hamish. 'I would have thought you would have kept them at home.'

'The reason I did not,' said Mrs Battersby, 'is because of the great responsibility of it all. If any went missing in my home, then I would get the blame.'

'There's a lot o' wickedness around,' said Willie. 'The minister was saying only last Sunday that it creepeth like the serpent and stingeth like the adder.'

'That's booze, not burglary,' snapped Hamish, distressed at this evidence that the minister was still reading out ancient hell-fire sermons.

There was a small group of women outside the church hall, headed by Mrs Wellington, her face white with distress.

'Who could have done such a thing?' she cried when she saw them.

'Chust let me see where the money was kept,' said Hamish.

Mrs Wellington produced a massive key and unlocked the church hall. She led the way into the kitchen and opened a cupboard under the sink. There, among the cleaners and dusters, was a tin box with a small padlock. The padlock had been broken.

'Now that's verra interesting,' said Willie.

'What is?' demanded Hamish.

'Judge's Lemon Shine,' said Willie, holding up a bottle. 'That'll no' get ye verra far with the cleaning, ladies. It's no good with the grease.'

'Get out of the way,' muttered Hamish, exasperated. He took a large handkerchief out of his pocket and gently lifted the box up on to the kitchen counter. 'Any sign of a break-in?' he asked. 'Any broken windows?'

'Nothing at all,' said Mrs Battersby.

'So who's got the key to the hall?'

There was a shamefaced silence and then one woman said, 'It's kept under the doormat outside. Anyone could have got it.'

'There's not much I can do, ladies,' said Hamish, 'short of fingerprinting the whole village, and even then I doubt if I'd find the prints of the thief on the box. There's probably only your fingerprints on it, Mrs Battersby.'

A small, angry-looking woman, Mrs Gunn, said, 'I notice ye got a new microwave the last week, Mrs Battersby.'

'What are you saying?' squeaked Mrs Battersby. 'Me, that's worked so hard for Famine Relief, to take that money!'

'We won't get to the bottom of this if you're all going to maliciously accuse each other,' said Hamish sharply. 'Now the money was all right on Sunday. This is Wednesday. Who's been in the hall since then?'

'The Guides used it on Monday evening,' volunteered Mrs Wellington, 'and the Boy Scouts on Tuesday evening.'

'Bessie Dunbar's the Guide captain,' said

Mrs Gunn, 'and herself came back from Inverness on Monday wi' a new coat.'

'Enough!' roared Hamish, upset by the malice, upset by the fact that the usually indomitable Mrs Wellington had begun to cry. 'I need a list of all the members of the Mothers' Union. Willie, you start taking statements from those here. Mrs Wellington, go home and get a cup of tea or something and I'll call on you later.'

By the end of the day, Hamish thought wearily that some of the murder cases he had previously worked on had been clean and innocent compared to the spite and malice roused by the theft of the Mothers' Union funds. Everyone seemed eager to accuse everyone else. Any woman who had a new purchase of any kind was evidently suspect. He doggedly went round the village taking statement after statement, ending up at the manse with Mrs Wellington.

'This iss a bad business,' mourned Hamish. 'I thought ye were all such friends, and now one's accusing the other.' He turned on the minister, who was slumped in an armchair by the fire. 'This village is in sore need of a lecture on common decency. I suggest you start thinking of them and less about yourself and give them a sermon about the wickedness of bearing false witness against their neighbour. I neffer thought to see the day in Lochdubh. If

I believed in the devil, then I'd say he'd come among you!'

'Maybe he has,' said Mrs Wellington, scrubbing at her red eyes with a damp handkerchief.

'Havers,' snorted Hamish. 'Where are the funds now?'

'Nobody trusts poor Mrs Battersby or anyone else,' said Mrs Wellington. 'So I took what's left to the bank and lodged it with the manager.'

Hamish asked a string of questions, trying to find out if anyone from outside had been seen in the village, but there was no one. There were guests up at Tommel Castle Hotel who had arrived on Sunday, but none as yet had come down to the village, the guests having been out on the river on the colonel's estate, fishing.

At last he made his way from the manse and then stopped in surprise outside the trim cottage owned by Jessie and Nessie Currie. A 'For Sale' sign was placed by the garden gate.

Now the sisters, although often a pain in the neck to Hamish with their frequent remarks that he was a lazy lout, *were* Lochdubh, as much a part of the scenery as the twin mountains which rose above the village, and the sea loch in front of it.

He had interviewed them earlier, for both, although spinsters, were members of the

Mothers' Union. He walked up to the door and knocked.

A lace curtain twitched beside the window and then there was a long silence. He knocked again. Jessie answered the door. 'Oh, it's yourself,' she said. 'It's yourself.' Jessie often repeated herself, like the brave thrush, as if she never could recapture the first fine careless rapture of her original sentences.

'You didnae tell me you were thinking of moving,' said Hamish.

'Why should we? Why should we?' demanded Jessie and then slammed the door in his face.

Hamish walked sadly away.

He was hailed by Dr Brodie. 'I'm going to the pub for a dram,' said the doctor. 'Care to join me?'

'Aye, I'd be glad to get the taste of this day out of my mouth.'

'I heard what happened,' said Dr Brodie. 'First the morphine and then this theft of money and the only people who might have taken the stuff are Sean and Cheryl, but the drugs weren't found on them and they were definitely out of the village when the money was stolen.'

'Everything's gone bad and wrong,' mourned Hamish. 'You should have heard these women, all hinting that one or the other one of them had stolen the funds. Jessie and Nessie Currie have put their house up for sale.'

'What?' The doctor stopped short in amazement. 'Why? What's happened?'

'I don't know. Jessie answered the door but she wouldn't talk to me. Everyone in this village has changed for the worse since Sean arrived.'

They walked into the bar. Dr Brodie bought two double whiskies and they sat down at a small table in the corner. The juke-box was belting out a country-and-western number which eventually twanged to a halt, leaving a blessed silence.

'Angela's gone funny again,' said the doctor.

'But she's been doing so well, studying for her degree,' said Hamish, 'and she's been so happy.'

'She's gone edgy of late and she keeps asking me for money for clothes. Angela! I could have sworn Angela didn't know what was on her back half the time. Do you know, Hamish, she came back from Inverness last week with a dress that cost three hundred pounds! Three hundred! I didn't know there was a shop in Inverness that sold anything as expensive as that.'

'Oh, Inverness is a boom town,' said Hamish. 'There's all sorts of shops now. Maybe we're behind the times. Maybe three hundred pounds is not an odd price for a frock.'

'Maybe not in Bond Street, but it's a hell of a price to pay for something to wear around the hills and glens.'

'Is it a verra grand frock?

'I'm no judge. It's just black, and the only thing about it is that it's got a Christian Dior label.'

'Are you worried she's fallen in love with someone else?' asked Hamish.

'There can't be anyone else. If you're thinking of Sean Gourlay, forget it. Oh, she took the odd cake and things over to the bus, but then she's like that. Always ready to welcome any newcomer to the village. But after the initial visits, she lost interest. There's something secret and nervy about her. I got out my torch and examined her eyeballs in case she had been taking the drugs for herself.'

'Well, that's enough to put any woman off her husband, for a start,' said Hamish.

'Aye, but I had to *know*. It's not drugs. She's plain miserable. One minute she's all over me, and the next, she's telling me to get lost.'

'Sean Gourlay . . .' began Hamish.

'Forget it,' sighed Dr Brodie. 'Admit it, you've had a bee in your bonnet about that one since he came here.'

'But everything's gone wrong since he came here,' protested Hamish. 'Everything's wrong, everything's polluted. Mr Wellington's lost his faith and is ranting rubbish from the pulpit which was written in the last century, and he doesn't believe a word of it. Mrs Wellington's a wreck, Jessie and Nessie are selling up, and the women at the Mothers' Union are that spiteful, you wouldnae believe it. There's something at the back of it all, and I mean to find out!'

The next morning, Sean and Cheryl returned. The next afternoon, they had a public row on the waterfront. Cheryl called Sean every name under the sun. She was astride the scooter and had a rucksack on her back. The fluency of her obscenities amazed the villagers, the mothers clamping their hands over their children's ears but continuing to listen themselves.

Shorn of obscenities, Cheryl's complaint was that she was sick of the village and sick of Sean and she was leaving and she would not be back.

Sean shrugged and smiled lazily and then loped off with long strides, up towards the manse. Cheryl drove off on the scooter, put-putting her way out of Lochdubh, over the newly repaired hump-backed bridge, up the long road which led past Tommel Castle Hotel and out of sight.

One down, thought Hamish Macbeth savagely, and one to go.

Chapter Five

There's a great deal to be said
For being dead.
   – E C. Bentley

After a week of squally, sleety rain, the weather became balmy again and the waters of the loch still. Sea-gulls cruised lazily overhead, swooping occasionally to admire their reflections and then soaring effortlessly up again. On the surface, Lochdubh looked much the same as ever. Smells of strong tea and tar and peat smoke. Sounds of radio, clattering dishes, bleating sheep, and chugging boats.

But underneath it all the theft of the Mothers' Union funds spread like a cancer. Hamish, after wondering how long Priscilla meant to ignore him, eventually caved in and took the single-track road up out of the village to the hotel.

He felt a slight pang when he saw her busy in the gift shop, her smooth blonde hair lit by a shaft of sunlight. She was selling expensive souvenirs to a group of men who, Hamish noticed with irritation, were taking a long time about their purchases.

At last the shop was empty. Priscilla gave Hamish a guarded look and said, 'Coffee?'

'That would be grand. Haven't seen you around for a bit.'

'I've been here, you know,' said Priscilla with an edge on her voice. 'I gather you and Doris had a pleasant dinner last week.'

'*She* invited me,' said Hamish defensively, for he felt guilty at having accepted the invitation, knowing he had only done it in the hope that Doris would tell Priscilla, which she evidently had.

Priscilla handed him a mug of coffee. 'Well, let's hope our new receptionist doesn't fall for you as well.'

'New receptionist? What's happened to Doris?'

'Dear me. Didn't she tell you? She left. She's got a job in a hotel in Perth.'

Hamish felt nothing but relief. Doris had all but proposed to him and it had been an agonizing and embarrassing evening.

'Well, what's been going on?' asked Priscilla. 'I heard about the money disappearing from the Mothers' Union.'

'Oh, it's the bad business.' Hamish pulled a chair up to the counter and sat down. 'All the women are at each other's throats, the one accusing the other. Dr Brodie's had four packets of morphine stolen and the only suspect was Sean, but he was searched and we couldn't find anything. His girlfriend's gone off but the bastard's still there, like some canker in the middle of the village.'

'It's those demonic good looks of his, Hamish. He's just a small-time crook, not the devil. I know he took that scarf and then slipped it back somehow.'

'He's doing a rare job, nonetheless. He's managed to talk Mr Wellington out of his faith and Mr Wellington has been using some old sermons he found and it's all hell-fire and damnation and they love it. Archie Maclean told me he gave up seeing a video of *The Werewolf Women of Planet Xerxes* because, to quote him, "the kirk was better fun". You should hear those sermons. A real medieval hell, wi' devils and pitchforks and weeping and wailing and gnashing of teeth. I tried to get him to talk to the priest, I tried to get him to preach kindness and love thy neighbour, but the man's sunk in gloom. Mrs Wellington looks a wreck. Nessie and Jessie Currie are selling up and leaving, and what that's got to do with Sean I don't know, but I feel it has. Angela Brodie's gone on the twitch again and this time is spending a fortune on clothes.'

'It sounds awful. How's Willie?'

'I don't know whether the lad's smitten with Lucia Livia, or whether it's the dirty stoves at the restaurant he's after. He lives to clean. Look at that!' Hamish held up one glittering black boot for her inspection. 'Even the insoles are polished. Look at my shirts! Starched, every one of them. I've got such knife-edged creases in my trousers, it's a wonder I don't cut myself.'

'Some people would think you were lucky,' pointed out Priscilla, 'living as you do with a combination of housekeeper and valet.'

'No, it iss not! I sat down to my breakfast this morning and Willie screeches, "A fly! A fly!" seizes a can of fly-killer and pumps it all over the kitchen and all over my food. If they ever take a blood sample from me, it'll be three parts insecticide and one part disinfectant. But I've got used to Willie. He's a kind enough lad. He's jist stark-staring mad, that's all. No, I feel if I could sort Mr Wellington out and get him to put some sense into the villagers, things would get better.'

'I'll see what I can do,' said Priscilla, unhitching her coat. 'I'm just about to lock up for lunchtime anyway.'

'You? What can you do?'

'He might just listen to me. It's worth a try.'

'Well,' said Hamish doubtfully, 'do your best. Have you forgiven me?'

'For letting Blair get away with all sorts of mayhem? I still think that was bad of you, Hamish, but when have I ever been able to stay mad at you for long?'

'It's a long time since you've been to see me.'

'I'm an old-fashioned girl. The gentlemen are supposed to call on me.'

'Well, I'll call on you tonight and take you for dinner.'

'Can't. The hotel's too busy. Sunday's free. Let's catch the hell-fire sermon and then go to the Napoli.'

'Suits me. But see if you can do something with Mr Wellington!'

Priscilla found the minister in his study. He was sitting in front of the fire, reading a book. 'Oh, Miss Halburton-Smythe,' he said in a dull voice, 'what can I do for you?'

'I've been hearing about you from Hamish,' said Priscilla.

The minister gave her a tortured look. 'Ah, yes,' he said with a weary sigh, 'about my loss of faith.'

'I am more concerned about you losing your marbles,' said Priscilla incisively.

He turned his head away. 'There is so much suffering in the world,' he moaned, 'and what can I do about it?'

'You could do something with your own parish. If everyone did some good about themselves, their family and their neighbours, the ripples might begin to spread outwards. I spoke to several of the village women before I came here. The place is riddled with spite. Instead of being sunk in self-absorption and self-pity, you might get off your bum and write a sermon to change the horrible spite and gossip of your parishioners. If you want your faith to come back to you, then you might start by acting as if you've got a heart and soul!'

Mr Wellington's head jerked round and he glared at Priscilla. 'There has often been talk that you might marry Hamish Macbeth,' he said, 'but now I think I know why the man is so reluctant to propose.'

'Why, you old horror!' said Priscilla, quite unruffled.

He rose to his feet. 'How dare you attack a minister of the Church!'

'Take a look at yourself in the mirror,' said Priscilla. 'Take a good hard look and then ask yourself if you are not looking at the most selfish man in the whole of Lochdubh. Forget about your lost faith. If it's such a terrible thing, don't you think you might try instilling some thoughts of faith, charity, and goodness into your flock? Why should they lose their faith, just because you've lost yours? I am going to hear your sermon on Sunday and I warn you, if you start reading out one of those old sermons, I will get to my feet and attack you in the middle of the church for being a fraud.'

She marched out. Hamish was strolling along the waterfront. He came up to her. 'How did you get on?' he asked.

'All right. I think a few gentle words were all that was needed.'

The church was crowded as usual on Sunday. Priscilla and Hamish managed to find space in a pew at the back. 'Look,' said Priscilla, nudging Hamish. 'There's your devil.'

Sean Gourlay was standing beside a pillar at the side of the church but where he could command a good view of the pulpit. He was wearing a black shirt and black cords. His odd green eyes glittered strangely in the light.

'Come to see his handiwork,' muttered Hamish.

There were hymns, a reading from the New Testament, and then the minister leaned forward over the pulpit.

A rustle of papers as peppermints were popped in mouths and then the congregation settled back to enjoy what Archie Maclean called 'a guid blasting'.

In a quiet, carrying voice, the minister began to talk of the theft of the funds. Sean crossed his arms and looked amused. The minister went on to say that this had caused malice and gossip in the village, turning one family against the other. His voice rose as he begged them to love their neighbour as themselves. His whole sermon seemed to be spoken directly to Sean. He spoke of the suffering in the world and reminded them that Jesus Christ had died on the cross for them. He said that the suffering in the village had been brought about by themselves. They had let one common theft poison their lives. 'There is no place for evil in this village,' he said. 'Look into your hearts and pray for charity, pray for kindness, and pray to the Good Lord for forgiveness for your sins. Let us pray together.'

Before he bent his head, Hamish noticed Sean walking quickly out of the church. It was silly, he told himself, to be so worried about one mere mortal, to be so superstitious, but somehow the minister's confrontation with Sean, and that was surely what it had been, reminded him of old tales he had heard when he was small in the long dark winter evenings of the black devil in man's form, walking into a Highland village one day and causing ruin and disaster.

A very subdued congregation shuffled out of the church. Mrs Gunn shook hands with Mrs Wellington and said they must think up a scheme to raise money to restore what had been taken and another woman patted Mrs Battersby on the back and said she had been doing a grand job as treasurer and hoped she would go on doing so. Groups of people were standing around the graveyard outside, talking to each other.

Hamish shook Mr Wellington's hand and said, 'A grand sermon.'

'Thank you,' said the minister. Then he suddenly added, 'Do not worry about Sean. I have a feeling he will be leaving us.'

'And what was that supposed to mean?' asked Hamish over lunch. 'Knowledge or the second sight?'

'I think, like you, he's decided Sean is the real reason for all the misery. When you think of it, who else could have taken that money?'

'But he and Cheryl weren't even here!'

They could have slipped back during the night. It's a simple matter to find the key and open up the village hall.'

'Well, let's hope the minister's right. If Sean doesnae move on, I'll need to think of some way to get him moving! What did you say to Mr Wellington to get him to see sense?'

'Just a few gentle and womanly words,' said Priscilla.

Hamish looked at her with admiration. 'Aye, it's a grand thing, a woman's touch,' he said. 'I must have been ower-blunt.'

* * *

Mr Wellington returned to the manse after evening service feeling comforted. By next week, he knew, his congregation would have dwindled to the usual small number, but instead of giving them what they wanted, he had given them what they sorely needed to hear. His wife had taken sleeping pills and gone to bed. He stared at the bulk of her sleeping form uneasily. She was taking a lot of sleeping pills these days.

He slept restlessly that night. At two in the morning, he got up to go to the bathroom. On his way, he peered out of a passage window which overlooked the manse field at the back. All the lights in the bus were blazing. He gave a little sigh. Supplying Sean with free electricity had been his wife's idea. She would have to tell Sean that they could do it no longer. He would speak to her in the morning, although it would be a difficult scene. Hamish had told her, he knew, about Sean's criminal record, but she had refused to take it seriously.

In the morning, on his way to the bathroom to shave, he once more looked out. It was a dark rainy morning and the lights were still blazing in the bus.

So when his wife tottered to the breakfast table, he snapped at her. 'Get dressed and tell that young hooligan that you befriended that he is no longer to use our electricity. In fact, while you are at it, you can tell him to go. I am not letting him use the field any more.'

'But you said you were in sympathy with these travellers,' she protested.

'I've been a fool, but no longer. Go and give that young man his marching orders.'

'I c-can't!'

His normally domineering wife was looking grey and crumpled.

Worry for her made him, like most husbands, angry instead of sympathetic.

'Don't be silly. If it makes you feel any better, tell him *I* am ordering him to go!'

Mrs Wellington eventually, encased in a voluminous waxed coat and rain-hat and Wellington boots, walked across the wet field to the bus.

She could hear the chatter from the television set inside. She knocked at the door and waited.

'Sean,' she called tremulously, and knocked again.

No answer.

She longed to turn away, to forget about the whole thing, but her husband would want to know why. She knocked loudly this time and then, in sudden desperation, sudden longing to get the whole distasteful business over with, she rattled the handle of the door. It swung open.

'Look here, Sean . . .' she began, heaving her bulk inside.

She stopped short and her mouth opened in a soundless scream.

Sean Gourlay lay on his back on the floor. His face and head had been beaten to a pulp. Beside him on the floor lay a bloody sledge-hammer. On the table, on the small television screen, a woman chattered in that inane way early-morning presenters have, as if address-ing an audience of children.

Mrs Wellington backed to the door. Small thin sounds were issuing from her mouth. She felt faint but dared not faint and be found lying next to that . . . that *thing*.

She stumbled from the bus and weaved her way like a drunk across the field. She opened the back door of the manse and the sight of home and familiar objects loosened her vocal cords and she threw back her head and gave a great cry of 'MURDER!' And once started, she could not stop.

Hamish Macbeth stood miserably in the manse field in the driving rain, with Willie beside him, while a forensic team went over the bus inch by inch. Detective Chief Inspector Blair was pacing up and down, wearing a deer-stalker and an old Inverness cape, looking like someone in an amateur production of a Sherlock Holmes mystery. The only thing that was lightening Blair's gloom was the fact that it was a nice seedy murder: no toffs involved. Just a hippie with his head bashed in. He'd had a public row with his girlfriend, the girl-friend had killed him, it was only a matter of time before they picked her up. He loathed being back in Lochdubh, a locality he associ-ated with success for Macbeth and failure for himself. There was no need for either Hamish or his sidekick to be hanging about in the rain, but Blair had kept them there to make them suffer; but as trickles of water began to run down inside his collar, he realized he was suf-fering as well and suggested they go back to the police station and discuss the matter there and let the forensic boys get on with their job.

'Well,' began Blair, pausing for a moment in surprise as Willie put a coaster under his coffee cup, 'it's straightforward enough. This creep has a row wi' his lassie, lassie comes back and bang, crash, goodbye boyfriend.'

'Was it murder wi' intentions?' asked Willie eagerly.

'If ye mean was her intention tae bash his head in, yes, you moron. Now the pathologist says death came frae thae blows from the sledge-hammer. Sledge-hammer belongs tae the manse. Whit dae ye think, Sergeant, that yer minister friend was at the sauce and slammed Sean Gourlay's head in?' Blair laughed heartily.

Hamish looked at him bleakly, his thoughts racing. He found he was hoping against hope that the murderer *was* Cheryl but for reasons he could not explain.

He began to give Blair a report on Sean's criminal background, reminding him of the theft of the morphine and the theft of the church money, although adding that both Sean and Cheryl had been away from the village when the money was taken.

The police station was pleasantly warm and Willie's coffee was good. 'I'd best jist sit here by the phone,' said Blair, 'while you two go off and take statements. I want to know anyone who saw hide or hair of Cheryl Higgins or anyone who heard the sound of that scooter you were talking about during the night.'

Hamish and Willie agreed to divide the village between them, Willie eagerly volunteering for the part which contained the Italian restaurant.

Despite the rain, little groups of people were standing about, peering anxiously up the hill towards the field at the back of the manse.

All day long, Hamish questioned and questioned, but no one had seen Sean after he had left the church and no one had seen Cheryl. Mrs Wellington had given the police a photograph of Cheryl which she had taken shortly after the couple had first arrived. It was shown on the six o'clock news. By seven o'clock,

Cheryl Higgins had walked into the police station at Strathbane, and Blair, hearing about it, had driven back to headquarters. By nine o'clock, Detective Jimmy Anderson phoned Hamish.

'Bad news,' he said. 'Cheryl Higgins has a cast-iron alibi.'

'She can't have,' exclaimed Hamish.

'Aye, but she has. She's been staying with a bunch of travellers in a field outside Strathbane and she's been playing the guitar in a group called Johnny Rankin and the Stotters – she being one o' the Stotters. The pathologist is checking the contents of Sean's stomach and he says the man was killed at a rough guess between ten in the evening and midnight. Cheryl was playing in Mullen's Roadhouse, you know, about two miles outside the town, from nine till one in the morning. Then she went on frae there to a party in Strathbane. Witnesses all along the way.'

'But how reliable are the witnesses?' asked Hamish. 'Stotter means glue-sniffer, doesn't it? Is that how the group got its name?'

'Probably. Most o' them were away wi' the fairies when we tried to talk to them, but there was the audience, about forty decent, or fairly decent, witnesses. She could ha' slipped away from the party, for I don't know if any of that lot knew whether they were coming or going, but the point is the time of the murder and

103

during that time she was performing in front of about forty people at the Roadhouse.'

'I'm surprised any band is allowed to play on the Sabbath in Strathbane,' observed Hamish.

'It's outside the town, so nobody bothers.'

'So where's this field she's living on?'

'On the Dalquhart Road out on the north side, about five miles out on the left. Belongs to Lord Dunkle, him what had the pop festivals back in the sixties. Still thinks he's a swinger, silly auld scunner that he is. She's living in a caravan with a couple called Wayne and Bunty Stoddart, old friends from Glasgow. She disnae look at all like the picture the minister's wife gave us, but it's her, all right. She's dyed her hair orange since the photo was taken. In Cheryl's humble opinion some bampot in Lochdubh upped wi' the sledgehammer and give him fifty whacks, and good riddance to bad rubbish, she says.'

'Did she suggest anyone?'

Anderson chuckled. 'Aye, she did that.'

'Who?'

'Sergeant Hamish Macbeth.'

'Silly bitch.'

'I'm telling you, that pleased Blair no end.'

Hamish sighed. 'So I suppose Blair'll be back tomorrow?'

'No, it'll be me and Harry MacNab. There's been a big robbery at the home of one of the super's friends, so Blair's jumped at that. He

104

disnae care about the death o' a layabout. No press coverage in it for him.'

'There's been a fair amount of press about today,' said Hamish.

'Aye, but they willnae be there tomorrow. Nobody in that village of yours had a good word to say for Sean Gourlay. If they had all said something nice, then the press could have run a "much-loved" type o' bit. Even the *Strathbane and Highland Gazette* have dropped it in case anyone remembers their touching piece about what a charming couple Sean and Cheryl were and being hounded by the nasty cops. They've found out from you and then Blair that Sean had a record.'

'Any relative to claim the body?'

'Got a mother in London, respectable body by all accounts. Coming up tomorrow to see the procurator fiscal.'

'I'm surprised the villagers turned out to be so down on Sean. All I got when the couple first arrived was about the romance of the road and leave the poor souls alone.'

'Believe me, the romance wore off, or maybe it's now that he's murdered and his past has come out, none of them want to confess to having had a liking for him. But you see what this means, Hamish?'

'I don't want to.'

I can see that. It means that mair than likely someone in Lochdubh did it.'

Hamish groaned.

'Cheer up,' said Anderson. 'You might find an itinerant maniac, if you're lucky.'

Hamish said goodbye and replaced the receiver. He pulled forward a sheet of paper. He would need to start with any villagers who had been on friendly terms with Sean. Top of the list were Mr and Mrs Wellington. Then Angela Brodie had been seen visiting the bus. Then came Nessie and Jessie Currie.

He sat back and looked dismally at the short list. He would need to detach his mind from the sore fact that these people were friends. So what had he?

Mr Wellington: lost his faith after a discussion with Sean and started preaching old sermons.

Mrs Wellington: nervous and agitated and not at all anything like her old, confident, bossy self.

Angela Brodie: acting strangely and buying expensive clothes.

Nessie and Jessie Currie: house up for sale, tetchy and miserable.

Well, forget about the murder, he would have to try to find out what Sean had done to these people. In the meantime, Willie could forgo his visits to the Napoli and keep questioning and asking in case anyone had seen a stranger that day.

Chapter Six

Suspicion all our lives shall be stuck full of eyes.
— Shakespeare

Despite Blair's lack of interest, the police were doing a thorough job. The forensic team came back to go over the bus again, inch by inch. The sledge-hammer was identified as belonging to the manse, but the bus was also full of items which Sean had borrowed from the Wellingtons. Mr Wellington said the sledge-hammer was normally lodged in a shed at the end of his garden. He was not aware that Sean had borrowed it at any time. Hamish had had high hopes for that hidey-hole under the bus, but it turned out to be full of the same bits of rubbish as before. In a neutral voice, he told Harry MacNab and Jimmy Anderson of the women who had been friendly with Sean, relieved in a way that the detectives would be questioning them and not himself. Never before had he been so reluctant to investigate

107

any case. Still, he could not resist asking them at the end of the day how they had got on.

'They're all white and shaken,' said Anderson, 'but that could be because of the shock. I mean, you've known all these women for some time now, Hamish, and you can hardly say that any one of them have shown criminal tendencies.'

'Forget about the women; what about the minister?'

'Nice old boy, but odd, really odd. He said something about the hammer of God.'

'He was probably quoting Chesterton,' said Hamish, who had read the Father Brown stories.

'Whoever he was quoting, he seemed smug. He said he'd called on the Lord for help and the Lord had helped, that sort of thing. Was he always that daft?'

'Not that I ever guessed,' said Hamish bleakly. 'Did you tell the Currie sisters they would have to stay in the village until the investigation was over?'

'Why? I thought a trip to Inverness was a big adventure for that pair.'

'Their house is up for sale.'

'Not now, it isn't,' said Anderson.

'So,' said Hamish, 'they were going to leave, Sean gets murdered, and they change their minds. Why?'

'Look, Hamish, I know you like these

people, but you know more about them than anyone else, and you're going to have to ask some questions yourself.' Anderson was lying back in a chair in the police station office, with his feet on the desk. Willie came in with a tray of coffee cups, clucked in disapproval, put down the tray, picked up a newspaper and slid it under Anderson's feet.

'That's mair like a houseboy than a policeman,' snorted MacNab when Willie had left the room, 'but he makes a grand cup o' coffee.'

'And there was nothing in the bus,' pursued Hamish, 'nothing at all.'

'Not a clue,' said Anderson. 'No morphine, no hundred pounds, no letters.'

'So what happens to the bus now?'

'Sean's mither phoned Mr Wellington and said she was too distressed over her son's death to do anything about it at the moment, and so Mr Wellington said the bus could stay where it was until she felt fit enough to come up and take it away, or any of his belongings. There'll be no trouble about it. Sean left a will, all right and proper, leaving everything to his mither.'

'Odd,' muttered Hamish. 'Any more on his background?'

'Oh, aye, this'll set you back. He was in the Hong Kong police for about six months but got the push.'

'Why?'

'Downright laziness. Should ha' been a man after your own heart, Hamish.'

'But this lassie, Cheryl,' pursued Hamish. 'Is there any way o' shaking her alibi?'

'Not with about forty witnesses to say she was in Mullen's the whole evening.'

'Damn, I'd like a word with her myself.'

'That'd be stepping out of your parish. You cannae shake that alibi.'

'Maybe. But I'd like to try all the same.'

Anderson sighed and poured more coffee. 'I think this is one case you're never going to solve, Hamish Macbeth. I feel it in ma bones.'

And so it seemed, as the days dragged into weeks. The file on Sean Gourlay was not closed, but it might just as well have been. The bus remained up on the field at the back of the manse, a daily mute reminder to Hamish of failure. He had interviewed the Wellingtons, Angela Brodie and the Currie sisters several times, but there was no change in their statements. They had gone out of their way to welcome Sean and Cheryl to the village and then had ceased to see them. They had been nowhere near the bus on the night of the murder.

He decided in despair to risk the wrath of Strathbane and go over on his day off and see if he could talk to Cheryl.

He went to Mullen's first. A sprawling red brick building with a huge car park, it was open twenty-four hours. A poster advertising various groups that neither Hamish nor possibly anyone else had ever heard of was pasted up on one of the windows.

Hamish pushed open the door and went in. It was a monument to the age of plastic: plastic plants trailed plastic fronds from plastic flower-boxes; plastic-covered chairs crouched beside low plastic tables. Even the long bar was made of plastic painted to look like wood. Hamish asked the barman for an orange juice and was mildly surprised to receive it in a glass tumbler instead of a plastic beaker. It was ten in the morning. A few couples were seated at the tables eating Mullen's Breakfast Special. Perhaps, thought Hamish, it was livelier in the evenings, with bands and crowds.

'Have you got Johnny Rankin and the Stotters playing here?' asked Hamish. 'I don't see them on the bill.'

'No' this month,' said the barman. 'Maybe next.'

'I've never heard of any of the groups you've got advertised,' said Hamish.

'Aye, weel, the manager books the cheap acts, that's why. Some of them are chronic.'

'Could I hae a word with the manager?'

'Who's asking?'

'Police,' said Hamish patiently, pointing to his uniform.

'Whit, again? Hang on a minute and I'll see if Mr Mullen's aboot.'

Hamish waited patiently. One customer shuffled over to the juke-box and dropped in some coins. Soon a pleasant tenor voice filled the room, singing 'Over the Sea to Skye', conjuring up Jacobite romance, far from the reality of this plastic road-house.

A small squat hairy man appeared behind the bar. He had very black eyes, like stones, and odd tufts of hair on his face, and hair sprouting from his nostrils and ears. He looked like a troglodyte squeezed into twentieth-century clothing.

'Mullen,' he said curtly to Hamish by way of introduction. 'What d'ye want?'

'I want to talk to you about Cheryl Higgins,' said Hamish.

'Oh, her! What can I tell you that I've no' said a'ready? She was here all right from nine till one in the morning, caterwauling away.'

'And you're sure it was her?'

'If you can find another lassie in the Highlands wi' thon orange hair, it'll be a miracle. No, it was her all right. Foul-mouthed creature, but then a lot of them are.'

'And she didn't leave the room at any time during the show?'

112

'Naw, that lot are like camels. Once they've got an audience, they can go on for hours and hours.'

Hamish thanked him and left, feeling depressed.

But he got into the police Land Rover and drove off in the direction of the travellers' campsite.

As he parked outside the field, he noticed the flurry of activity the sight of him caused. Weird figures were seen scuttling here and there, doors banged shut as children were scooped up and carried inside. It was as if a monster had arrived, but Hamish guessed they were probably hiding drugs or items of petty theft.

Only one woman stayed where she was, stirring something in a cooking pot over an open fire.

Hamish approached her. 'Where are the Stoddarts?' he asked. She was a thin, fantastically dressed creature, wearing a heather coronet on her tangled locks. A long Indian cotton dress hung about with beads and brooches was wrapped around her body. She turned pale dim eyes up to him and frowned as if he had asked her to expound Einstein's Theory of Relativity. 'The Stoddarts,' he prompted.

'Ower there,' she said, pointing in the direction of a small caravan painted bright blue.

Hamish walked up to it and knocked on the door. A vague-looking bearded man answered it.

'Mr Stoddart,' said Hamish, 'is Cheryl Higgin's here?'

'Come in,' he said and retreated back into the dimness of the caravan, which still had its curtains drawn closed. The confined space smelled of unwashed bodies. The bearded man joined a slattern of a girl, no doubt his wife, at a table at one end. Both were watching television on a small black-and-white set placed on the table. Hamish looked round. At the other end of the caravan was a bunk with a flaming-orange head poking above the pile of bedclothes. He went over.

'Cheryl,' he said.

She twisted round and looked up at him. Then her mouth opened and a stream of abuse poured out. Hamish waited patiently until she had run dry, guessing correctly that Cheryl's outpourings were part of a long-established pattern.

When she fell silent, he perched on the end of the bed and said quietly, 'Now you've got that out of your system, I want to ask questions about you and Sean, not the usual ones.'

She gazed at him sullenly.

'Why did you leave Sean?' asked Hamish.

'It wasnae any kind o' life,' she said bitterly. 'I think he wus screwed in the heid. He would

114

get visits from thae awful old women frae the village and ask me to take a walk and sometimes I couldnae get back to ma bed till after midnight.'

Hamish felt suddenly miserable. He did not want to ask any further questions but knew he had to.

'Who were these women?'

As if she sensed that he didn't really want to know, Cheryl brightened visibly and something like a look of satisfaction came into her eyes. 'Well, there was that fat Wellington cow, for one. "Dear Sean, I've just baked this cake specially for you." Ugh. Then there was a wee wumman wi' glasses who sounded like a jammed record.' Jessie Currie, thought Hamish. 'Aye, and the doctor's wife, too.'

'Anyone else?'

'Isn't that enough?'

'How often did Sean beat you?'

She sat up in bed and hugged her thin arms about her body. 'Get oot o' here,' she muttered.

'All right, I'll leave that question aside for the moment. Have you any idea what the relationship between Sean and these women was?'

'It couldnae hae been sex,' she jeered. 'He strung them along so he could get presents o' food and cakes.'

'Money?' asked Hamish sharply, remembering the missing hundred pounds.

'No,' she mumbled, her head going down again.

He tried and tried but Cheryl said she had nothing more to tell. As far as she knew, Sean enjoyed causing a flutter among the middle-aged women of the village, and yet Sean must have done something wrong, for after his death no one had a good word to say for him.

Hamish finally gave up and left. He stood outside the caravan and looked slowly around at the other caravans and ancient buses which were dotted about the field. He felt sad and weary and so had a sudden understanding of why these unlovely people stepped out of society and took to the road. No responsibilities, no rent, no jobs, unless playing the occasional gig could be called a job. No hard drugs; drink, glue, or hashish when they could get it. They helped each other out, romanticized their life-style, and often got other people to believe in that romance. Let other people pay the taxes to supply them with dole money, let other people build and maintain the roads they drove on, let other people clean up the mess they left behind; they were the Peter Pans who had found a way of never growing out of adolescence, and the rest of the world was one indulgent parent to see to their needs.

A small fine rain was scudding in on a warm west wind. The woman was still stirring that pot, although the fire had blown out. Hamish gave himself a mental shake. It was unlike him to stand moralizing in the middle of a damp field when he himself was hardly one of the world's exemplary workers.

So what had Sean done with the women? he wondered as he drove north again. Had he talked them into some sort of mental crisis, like the one he had inflicted on the minister? He had undoubtedly possessed a certain magnetism. But what had he done to drive someone to bashing his face and head in? It had been a murder done in pure hatred.

Mrs Wellington, Angela Brodie, and Jessie Currie would have to be questioned again, and this time without their minders: Mrs Wellington without the minister, Angela without Dr Brodie and Jessie without Nessie.

Evening was settling down on Lochdubh as he drove down the hill in the heathery twilight. The fishing boats were setting out to sea. Smoke rose lazily from chimneys and a group of children were playing on the beach, their cries as shrill as the calls of sea-birds. But the blackness, the malignancy that lay under it all would never go away unless he found out who had murdered Sean.

He went into the police station, thinking wryly that for all his impatience with Willie, he was becoming spoilt by being perpetually waited on.

But Willie was in the living room slumped in front of a television set. 'Where did that come from?' asked Hamish.

'Mr Ferrari,' said Willie dully. 'It's an auld one o' his. He's got one of the new ones. This one disnae have the remote control.'

'That's grand,' said Hamish. 'What's on?'

'I dinnae know and I dinnae care. I don't like television.'

Hamish sat down opposite him, first turning off the set.

'Out with it, Willie.'

'It's a serious matter and I don't want tae have to put up with your usual levitation.'

'No levity, I promise.'

'I was at the restaurant,' began Willie.

'You're always at that restaurant,' said Hamish impatiently.

Willie threw him a hurt look.

'I'm sorry,' said Hamish quickly. 'What happened? Was it anything to do with Lucia?'

Willie nodded.

'Did you make a pass at her and get your face slapped?'

Willie sat up straight. 'I would never lay a finger on that lassie if she didnae want it.'

'So, what's the problem?'

'I shouldnae hae been listening,' said Willie. 'Lucia said there was a new dish the cook, Luigi, wanted me to try. It was this morning and the restaurant wasn't opened yet. So I was

118

sitting at the table over by that auld fireplace and I could hear Mr Ferrari quite clearly. He was talking to someone in the room above, a man. I heard the name Sean Gourlay and that's when I started to listen.

'Mr Ferrari said, "Thon bastard's dead and gone, thank goodness. I'm glad I was saved from killing him myself." The other man said something I couldnae hear and then Mr Ferrari said, "After what he did to Lucia ..." And then I couldnae hear any mair.'

'So did you ask him about it?'

'I couldnae,' wailed Willie. 'If there was something between her and thon monster, I don't want tae know.'

'I'm beginning to think not knowing iss worse than anything else,' said Hamish, half to himself. 'Help yourself to a whisky, Willie. I'll ask Ferrari.'

'He'll know I was listening!' cried Willie.

'True, but I'll tell him you couldn't help it.'

As Hamish walked along to the restaurant, he turned over the names of the staff in his mind. There was old Mr Ferrari, and Lucia, who acted as waitress. Conchita Gibson, another distant relative who had married a Scotsman who had died of cancer the year before; Luigi, the cook; Giovanni, the under-cook; and Mrs Maclean, Archie the fisherman's wife, who came in daily to clean, made up the rest of the staff.

119

The restaurant was fairly busy, for its reputation had grown so much that many of the customers motored long distances to eat there and the prices were still low enough to tempt the locals.

Lucia welcomed Hamish with a dazzling smile. She really is a stunner, thought Hamish. Poor Willie. Not a hope in hell.

He asked for Mr Ferrari. Lucia disappeared and then returned and led him through the back of the restaurant and up a flight of stairs to the flat over the shop.

'Come in, Sergeant,' cried Mr Ferrari. 'Have a drink, but don't stay too long, because I've a lot to attend to.'

'No drink,' said Hamish, 'chust a few questions. Willie was here this morning.'

'Grand lad, that. Should be in the restaurant trade.'

'Maybe. The fact is he wass sitting next to the fireplace and he could hear something of what you were saying upstairs.'

All the wrinkles on Mr Ferrari's old face settled into a sort of hard mask from behind which his eyes peered warily out.

'All he could gather,' went on Hamish, 'wass that you were glad someone had killed Sean or you might have done it yourself after what he did to Lucia. Now who were you talking to and what did Sean Gourlay do to Lucia?'

'Like the television set?' asked Mr Ferrari.

'If that wass meant as a bribe, then you can be having it back!' exclaimed Hamish. Mr Ferrari looked at Hamish steadily.

'Don't you see you are making matters worse for yourself?' said Hamish. 'Tell me the truth.'

'And you will not tell anyone?' Mr Ferrari demanded.

'Not unless it's necessary, no.'

'It's not a nice story. Lucia does not go out walking with any man without my permission. Sean asked her to go for a walk with him, she asked me and I refused. I did not want her tied to anyone who showed no signs of wanting to work. But he was a regular customer, although where he got the money from, I don't know, and so he managed to speak to her . . . a lot. He was very handsome. So Lucia begged and begged to be allowed to go out with him, so I at last said she could on her day off, in the afternoon, but she was to be back at six o'clock. I sent Giovanni after them to keep watch. I tell you, Hamish,' he went on, 'I've met a lot of bad people in my long life, and I had Sean marked down as a real bad one. But I couldn't be sure. I kept wishing that wee lassie, Cheryl, had still been with him. Lucia wouldnae have dreamt of going out with him then.

'So off they went and Giovanni set out after them. All excited he was, dodging in and out of doorways with a cap down over his eyes and a scarf over his mouth, and then creeping up the hillside. I thought Sean was bound to notice the idiot, but as it turned out, he did not.

'They only went a little away up on the moor and they were sitting side by side on one of those big boulders. Giovanni crept up and lay in the heather behind them.

'Sean began telling Lucia she was the most beautiful woman he'd ever seen and she asked if he'd been in love with Cheryl and he gave her a spiel that Cheryl was a waif frae Glasgow he was being kind to and what had bit the hand that fed it and all that rubbish.

'Then he suggested she go back to that bus of his. He said he had some good videos. But she said it was their first time out and wasn't the view lovely and maybe another time and so on. Then he grabbed her and kissed her and Giovanni said he didn't know what to do because she was enjoying it and it was only kissing. Then Sean began to unbutton her blouse and Lucia pushed him off, but he tumbled her on to the ground and I believe Giovanni when he said it could have been rape if he hadn't been there. So Giovanni ups from the heather and shouts, 'Stop!'

'He said Sean looked like the very devil, those cat's eyes of his glittering in the light, and Lucia, she was crying her eyes out. Giovanni said he was right glad he'd taken the meat cleaver with him.'

Hamish suppressed a grin.

'So Sean saw that cleaver and began to run and Giovanni went after him and chased him right back to that bus. Then he told me. So we all went to see him, me and Luigi and Giovanni, and we told Sean Gourlay that if he came near the restaurant or Lucia ever again, we would cut his balls off. So that's it.'

'You should have told me this before,' said Hamish.

'Why?' demanded Mr Ferrari. 'None of us killed him.'

But Hamish left very worried. There was a field at the back of the restaurant and from the field it was possible to cut across the other fields and get to the one behind the manse. And yet how simple it would be for him if, say, Giovanni had done it. How he longed for an outsider. And yet, although Mr Ferrari and his relatives had only set up their restaurant a short time ago in the village, they had quickly become a valuable part of the local life. The small shack which served as a Catholic church was to be gradually replaced by a brick building, money supplied by Mr Ferrari. The restaurant had become a gathering place for local birthdays and wedding anniversaries.

At the police station, he told Willie what had happened. 'I should've been there,' said Willie. 'Not that Lucia cannae protect herself.'

'In what way?'

'She told me she was walking home and one o' the forestry lads grabbed her and tried to steal a kiss.'

'And?'

'She kicked him in the family silver.'

'You mean jewels.'

'Whatever.'

Could Lucia have done it herself? wondered Hamish. She had been keen enough on Sean to beg Mr Ferrari to let her go out with him. Was she one of the women who had gone to the bus? Cheryl wouldn't know, for Sean's pursuit of Lucia had started after Cheryl had gone.

He shook his head wearily. 'Did Mr Ferrari blame me for reporting it?' asked Willie anxiously.

Hamish shook his head. 'As long as you go on neglecting your duties and giving him free labour, he won't go off you.'

'It's not as if anything ever happens in Lochdubh,' said Willie sulkily.

'Except murder,' said Hamish.

Hamish set out the next day to try to get his female suspects alone. He waited until he knew Dr Brodie would be at the surgery and went to call on Angela. He felt a pang of worry when he saw her. It was like that time when that woman had been murdered in Lochdubh, he thought, and Angela, who had been under her influence, had mentally gone off the rails. She looked now as she had then, thin and brittle.

'Not more questions,' said Angela when she saw him.

'I have to keep asking,' said Hamish patiently. 'Can I come in?'

'I suppose so.' Angela led the way into the kitchen. The table was covered in textbooks. She shovelled a clear space at one corner and sat down. Hamish sat opposite her.

'I went to see Cheryl yesterday,' said Hamish. Angela pushed a tress of fine wispy hair out of her eyes. 'And?' she demanded.

'I gather that some evenings, Cheryl was sent out for a walk while Sean entertained some ladies. You were one of the ones mentioned. The previous times I've spoken to you, you've always said you went over with cakes and things when Sean and Cheryl originally came to the village, as a sort of welcome. You never said anything about spending any time with Sean alone.'

'I didn't want my husband to find out,' said Angela. 'All that happened was that I went over one evening to talk about my studies because he had seemed interested, and John never listens to me. When I talk about anything to do with this Open University degree, he switches off. Cheryl went out when I arrived. I stayed and talked, had a few drinks

125

and then left. I never went back again because I thought if John ever found out about it, it would . . . well . . . look odd.'

'And that's all there was to it?'

'Yes, Hamish, what else could there have been?'

'Sean didn't ask you for money or . . .' Hamish looked at her in growing concern . . . 'drugs?'

'I thought you were a friend, Hamish. How can you say such things?' Angela covered her thin face with her thin hands and began to cry.

'Now, now,' said Hamish awkwardly. 'Dinnae greet. I haff to ask these questions, you know that. Haven't you anything you'd like to get off your chest?'

'I'd like you to get out of here, *now*,' yelled Angela, her tear-stained face contorted.

Hamish rose to his feet and stood looking down at her. 'I'll go now,' he said heavily, 'but I'll have to be back.'

Priscilla, he thought, as he stood outside the doctor's house, I need Priscilla. He drove up to the hotel in time to catch her closing up the gift shop for lunch.

'Hello, Hamish,' she said, 'I'm just about to have lunch, coffee and sandwiches in the bar. You can join me, if you'd like.'

When they were seated in a corner of the bar, Hamish having agreed to coffee and refused whisky because he was driving, much as he would have liked one, for he had found the interview with Angela harrowing, Priscilla looked at him and said, 'This case is really getting you down. Want to talk about it?'

So he told her all he knew from the beginning, outlining his fear that the murder had been committed by someone from the village.

'I think we should write some of this down,' said Priscilla. She rose and went through to the reception desk and came back with several sheets of paper. 'Now,' she said, 'let's sort it out. All the women who have visited Sean have become wrecks. Mrs Wellington is a shadow of her former self. Angela is on the twitch and spending far too much money on clothes, which is totally out of character. The Currie sisters plan to sell up and move. Sean dies. They take the sign down.

'There's a common factor there, Hamish. You're normally so acute. You've missed it although it's been staring you in the face all the time because you're praying for some outsider to turn out to be the murderer.'

'And what's the common factor?'

Priscilla tapped the paper with her pen.

'Money,' she said. 'They all needed money. Perhaps not Mrs Wellington. But the rest badly needed money.'

Chapter Seven

O villain, villain, smiling, damned villain!
                              – Shakespeare

Hamish looked down at the paper, his mind scurrying this way and that, trying to find a road away from the three women.

Then he gave a sigh and leaned back. 'Aye, you're maybe right. But Angela now, she was spending money on *herself*, not Sean.'

Priscilla tapped the paper again. 'Drugs, Hamish. The missing morphine. And there's another thing.'

'What's that?'

'I called on Angela. She was wearing a black dress. I complimented her on it although I thought it made her look like a waiflike widow and she said uneasily that it had cost an awful lot of money, that it was a Dior.'

'So was it?'

'Yes, I should think it was – but a second-hand Dior.'

'How second-hand?'

'There were worn patches under the arms and although it was a simple style, it's very short in the skirt and I would guess it was about twenty years old.'

'What are you getting at?'

'There are thrift shops in Inverness, Hamish, where a woman can buy a model dress for a few pounds and then tell her husband it cost a fortune.'

Hamish looked at her miserably.

'Now, Hamish, it may not be any of them, but you'll never get to the bottom of it if you don't start finding out why they all needed money. Sean must have been blackmailing them.'

'And Sean is dead and they're all still worried, although the Currie sisters have decided to stay in Lochdubh,' said Hamish. 'And they are worried, which means they think perhaps Cheryl or someone might have got their hands on the blackmailing material. I'm going back for another look at that bus.'

'I notice it's still there,' said Priscilla. 'Wasn't there a mother or someone who was going to claim it?'

'Yes. Mrs Gourlay. She said she would be up next week to take a few things. She asked if anyone would want to buy the bus and I suggested she try Ian Chisholm at the garage. I'd better start work right away.'

'Could Willie help?'

'I doubt it. He's really lovesick now. Lucia's walking out with Tim Queen.'

'Oh, dear,' said Priscilla. Tim Queen was a handsome young man whose father owned the Lochdubh Bar.

'Aye, Willie skulks around after them, looking like a whipped dog.'

Walking out was an old-fashioned pastime, but there was little else for a courting couple to do in Lochdubh. Lucia and Tim Queen were leaning over the bridge, looking down at the River Anstey. Lucia kept flicking little speculative looks at Tim from under her long lashes. He was tall and red-haired, with a square, pleasant freckled face. The Lochdubh Bar, once an extension of the Lochdubh Hotel, which was still awaiting a buyer, had been bought by Tim's father in a separate sale and had been making a profit ever since.

Tim looked down at Lucia's small red hands, which were resting on the parapet of the bridge, and then covered one of them with his own. Lucia snatched her hand away.

'What's the matter?' asked Tim. 'I was only holding your hand.'

'I am ashamed of my hands,' said Lucia, putting them behind her back. 'They are so red. I would like soft white hands.'

'But that's what I like about ye,' said Tim

earnestly. 'You're an old-fashioned girl. I don't like the young ones round here who slap paint all ower their faces and never do a day's work and wouldnae know how to scrub a kitchen floor if you asked them.'

Lucia's beautiful eyes became clouded with sad thought. 'So you like a woman who does the housework, Teem?'

He slid an arm about her waist. 'Yes, that's my sort of girl. My friend, Johnny, over at Darquhart, just got married, and his wife, Darleen, well, she wanted a cleaning woman frae day one!'

'What is so odd about that?'

He laughed. 'You silly wee thing, why should Johnny pay for a cleaning woman when he's got a wife?'

She slid out from his arm and looked about. 'Why, there is Constable Lamont,' she cried.

She was looking at a stand of trees beside the river. Tim could not see anything.

But Lucia waved and sure enough, Willie eased out from behind a tree. 'Do not bother to walk back with me, Teem,' said Lucia gaily. 'See, I am safe with my policeman.'

And Tim never knew what he had said wrong.

Hamish collected the keys to the bus from the police station and then strode up to the field behind the manse. Sean's presence still seemed to be around the place. He had a superstitious feeling that he was still in the bus and would laugh at him when he opened the door.

The day was warm and overcast, with great clouds of midges dancing on the muggy air.

He unlocked the door of the bus and climbed inside.

Everything was as the forensic team had left it and as he had last seen it. He began to search methodically, but wondering all the time what he could find that an experienced forensic team had missed. He even opened packets of coffee and bags of sugar in the hope of discovering something hidden in them. He worked for hours and did not find one thing.

He sat down miserably on a bench at the side of the table and looked dully at the blank screen of the small television set. There were videos piled up in a heap at the end of the table. As a last hope, he slid them out of their packets. They were mostly of the brutal sex-and-violence kind, but nothing under the counter, nothing illegal. He sighed. Then suddenly a little picture came into his brain, a picture of Sean striding along the waterfront with that easy athletic pace of his, carrying a video camera. He looked wildly around. There was the television, there were the videos, there was the video recorder, but no camera. But Patel rented one out.

133

The bus was still hitched up to the manse electricity. He switched on the television set and began to feed the videos into the machine, fast-forwarding them through a series of murders and rapes and general mayhem. The weather was clearing outside and yellow sunlight suddenly flooded the interior of the bus. Children's voices drifted in along with the other homely sounds of the village, a different world from the misery of filth and violence which was flickering in front of him.

He ejected the one he had scanned through and put in another called *The Rage of the Mutants* and pressed the fast-forward button. Then, with an exclamation, he ran it back to the beginning and began to play it at normal speed. With a sinking heart, he found himself looking at Mrs Wellington. She was smoking and giggling and drinking. Hamish stopped the film and peered hard at that cigarette. It was a reefer, hash, grass. 'You do make me feel wicked,' Mrs Wellington burbled as he started the film again. Her eyes were glazing over. Sean's voice was only a mumble in the background. Then there was a long blank and suddenly a couple in an amorous embrace leaped onto the screen. Angela Brodie and Sean. His mouth was clamped over hers and one hand was stroking her breast and she was moaning in his embrace. Angela suddenly pulled free and the film went blank again. It ran on towards the end and then Hamish blushed. For there was Jessie Currie, stark-naked, roaring and laughing and holding a glass of something. And then the film finished.

Hamish sat back, sweating. It all fell into place: Mrs Wellington's distress and the missing money from the Mothers' Union, Angela and the second-hand dress and the missing morphine, Jessie and Nessie selling their house.

He should phone Strathbane and send them the video and let them take it from there. But he could not. Even if none of them had murdered Sean, their reputations would be in rags. Dr Brodie and Mr Wellington would have to know what their wives had been up to.

Hamish switched off the television set and put everything back in place, except the incriminating video, which he took with him. There must be some way round this. For a start, he would have to try to get the culprits alone.

He let himself out of the bus and carefully locked the door. He stood blinking in the late sunshine. A brisk wind was blowing and the midges had gone.

He had a sudden picture of Sean, smiling and lounging beside the bus, his hands thrust into his trouser pockets, and Hamish Macbeth felt that he could have murdered the man himself for wrecking such innocence. Hamish was sure Cheryl either did not know about the money or, if she had, had not been able to get any of it. If that was the case, it still had to be hidden somewhere. He looked slowly around. There was no outside toilet, and none on the bus. Sean had probably used one of the lavatories at the manse, the one situated just inside the back door. There was nothing outside except the packing case lying on its side, gaping empty, on which Sean and Cheryl had sat on the day he had come to search for morphine. He gave it a slight push and then peered inside. It was weighted down with rocks.

He placed the video carefully on the grass and crawled inside the packing case and dragged out the rocks. Then he pushed it aside. A square patch of bleached grass was revealed. He examined it closely and noticed that the square was made up of squares of long-grassed turf. Excited, he started to haul them up; a difficult job, for they had begun to grow together. Finally he got the last one clear and smiled with satisfaction. Buried underneath was a plastic rubbish bag full of something. He pulled it up and opened it. It was heavy but proved to be weighted with stones. But inside as well was a square cash box. The box was locked. 'Tampering with the evidence,' screamed a voice of warning in his head, but he shrugged it away and took out a set of skeleton keys from his pocket and got to work. It took some time and he was glad the bus screened him from the manse windows. Finally the lock clicked and he opened the lid. The box was stuffed with pound notes – fifties, twenties, tens and fives. Underneath lay four packets of morphine. He counted the money carefully. Just over a thousand pounds. Hardly blackmail on a grand scale. He carefully replaced everything and put the bag back in the hole and covered it over with the turf and the packing case and then crawled inside to replace the rocks. Once the rocks were pushed to the back, he realized that to the forensic team, they would not be visible and it would have simply looked to them like an empty packing case on its side, showing the world that there was nothing there.

He consoled himself with the thought that he could always pretend to find the stuff later. Right now, he meant to confront the women on that video. But how to get them alone?

Two days later, Angela Brodie opened a thin envelope and stared mesmerized at the thin typewritten slip inside. It said, 'Come to the police station at ten this morning. I have a film to show you. Hamish Macbeth.'

'What's that?' asked Dr Brodie. 'You look as if you've seen a ghost.'

'Nothing,' said Angela. 'I thought it was my exam results and got all upset, but it's just a note from Mrs Wellington. There's to be a meeting at the church hall to discuss raising funds.'

'Hope nobody pinches them again,' said the doctor, losing interest.

Mrs Wellington at that same moment was reading a note from Hamish Macbeth. She let out a squawk and her husband lowered his newspaper and looked at her impatiently. 'Another bill?' he asked.

'No, it's nothing,' she said, crushing the envelope and slip of paper in her large hand. 'Some Mothers' Union business. I've got to go out this morning.'

But the minister was once more reading his newspaper and did not seem to care.

Nessie Currie twitched the slip of paper out of her sister Jessie's trembling fingers.

'I'm ruined ... ruined,' whispered Jessie.

'You'll need to face up to him,' said Nessie. 'I'll come with you.'

'No, no. I'll need to go on my own, on my own. Everyone will find out, find out. I cannae stay here.'

'You have sinned against the Lord,' said Nessie, 'and you must take your punishment.' Then her face softened. 'I'll come along as well, Jessie. I'll stand by you. We'll face this together, and then we'll sell up and go far down south, Inverness or somewhere like that.'

Willie, delighted to have a morning off, had actually offered to take Towser for a walk. He had finally taken an odd liking to Hamish's yellowish mongrel of a dog, mainly because Lucia liked Towser and Towser had developed a taste for pasta.

Hamish had borrowed a video recorder from Mr Patel, not wanting to borrow the one from the bus in case anyone saw him with it and asked him what he was doing. Angela, Mrs Wellington and the Currie sisters arrived together.

Hamish silently ushered them into the living room, where they sat down with jerky movements, and all stared mesmerized at the still blank television screen.

Hamish slid the cassette into the recorder. He ran the film. When it had finished, he looked at them. Angela and Mrs Wellington were sitting together on the sofa, and they were holding hands. Nessie had an arm around Jessie's shoulders. But despite their distress and obvious strain, there was a faint air of surprised relief about them all. They were not alone, he realized, in their misery and shame, and that was the reason for the faint air of relief.

'The situation is this,' said Hamish. 'I have found the money and the morphine, but I cannot do anything about returning it. I should be down in Strathbane showing this video at headquarters. The reason I have not done so should be obvious to all of you. For some reason you let this man trick you and blackmail you. The only way out of it is to try to find the murderer and get the case closed.'

'But if you find the murderer,' said Angela in a croaky voice, 'it will all come out in court and the video will be shown as well.'

'Not necessarily. I am in as bad trouble as the rest of you, for I could easily lose my job for suppressing this evidence. If I find the murderer, it is possible I can do a deal. I will promise him or her not to mention the blackmailing so that charge will not be added on to the one of murder. But I'll never find out who murdered Sean unless everyone here tells the truth.' He turned to Angela. 'You first.'

She pushed her wispy hair back from her eyes. 'It was a sort of madness,' she said. 'He was so handsome. He made it clear that he had no interest in Cheryl, other than giving her a home, and I believed him. He was so interested in this degree I am studying for, the only person who has ever shown any interest.'

Except me, who pushed you into doing it, thought Hamish huffily.

'It was easy to forget Cheryl,' went on

Angela, 'because as soon as I arrived, she went out. I'd never even looked at any other man since I married John. Oh, I was flattered that such a young and good-looking man seemed to find me attractive. If he'd come on too strong at the beginning, I would have shied away, but I am very romantic and he used the romantic approach. He asked me to come one evening and said he had some films to show me. I told John I was going to see Mrs Wellington. Instead of any films, he produced a bottle of champagne. I'm not used to drinking – I had told him that – and I got drunk pretty quickly. We were sitting on that bench at the end of the bus. He began to kiss me and I . . . responded. And then I heard this whirring sound, very faint, and I looked down the bus and I could see the video camera propped on the table facing us and I realized it was running. I pushed him away and stumbled out of that bus and ran home and I vowed never to go near him again. I only thought he was weird because he was prepared to film our love-making without telling me.

'He stopped me in the street a few days later. He said he would show the film to my husband unless I paid him. John and I have a joint account. I panicked and said I couldn't. He laughed and told me to get him some morphine and then he would leave me alone.

'I took the keys to the surgery that night when John was asleep and got the drugs. I thought that would be an end of it, but next week he was back, asking for money. I was frantic with worry. He said he didn't want much. At first he asked for fifty, then it was a hundred, then another hundred, and so on. I pretended to John that I was buying expensive dresses in Inverness and paying cash for them when, in fact, I was buying them cheap from the thrift shops. I was so glad when I heard he was dead and then, when I realized the police would probably find that video, I was frightened to death all over again. Oh, Hamish, John must never find out.'

'I'll do my best,' said Hamish heavily. He faced Jessie. 'Now you.'

Jessie sobbed and stumbled over the words and repeated everything, but the sad story slowly emerged. She, too, had been flattered by the attentions of this young man. She had gone to the bus. He gave her something to drink and she didn't remember a thing after that until somehow she was in her own bed at home and Nessie was sitting next to her.

'He must have put something in her drink,' said Nessie, 'for she was raving and seeing things. I didnae call the doctor, thank the Lord for that, for I thought she maybe had the DTs and that would have been a shame and disgrace. When she told me she had had one drink and didn't remember anything after that, I didnae believe her. Then Sean Gourlay called, as bold as brass. He asked to see her alone. After he had gone, I could see she was frightened to death and so I got it out of her. He wanted twenty pounds. That's a lot for us. Dad left us the house and a bit in the bank, but just enough for us to get by on if we watch carefully. I told Jessie to give him the twenty but warned her he would probably be back. And so he was. So I said to Jessie we should sell up and get out of Lochdubh where he could never find us . . .' Her voice trailed off and she sat in dumb misery.

Oh, may you burn in hell, Sean Gourlay, thought Hamish. Jessie was probably, at the age of fifty-something, still a virgin. She and Nessie were staunch church-goers. No one would ever think, looking at the pair of them, that there would ever be anything about either of them to blackmail. They both had brown hair, permed ferociously into small tight curls, and thick glittering glasses and thin spare figures.

'Now, Mrs Wellington,' he said, 'what is your story?'

'He said they were Turkish cigarettes,' said Mrs Wellington bitterly. 'And how would I know any different? He made me feel young and reckless and I had *never* felt young or reckless before. I haven't even any children.'

143

Hamish did not feel like asking her what she meant by that. 'I married a suitable man and settled down to do good works. I was tired of good works,' she said, tears starting to her eyes, 'and now look what my wickedness has brought me to. I'm a silly old fool. I, like Mrs Brodie, have a joint account, and Mr Wellington checks it every week!' Hamish had always considered it odd that Mrs Wellington always referred to her husband as 'Mr Wellington', like a Victorian lady. 'I was so desperate, I thought if I gave him a big sum, he would go away. He *promised* to go away. I stole the money from the Mothers' Union. But he came back for more. I sold some of my jewellery to keep him quiet. When he died, I was so glad it was all over.'

'And did any of you kill him?' asked Hamish.

'No,' said Mrs Wellington.

'No,' squeaked Jessie.

'I wanted to,' said Angela heavily. 'I dreamt about it every day. But I didn't kill him. What happens now, Hamish?'

'I'll need to keep this evidence here, in my room where Willie won't find it, and then try to see Cheryl again. She must have known about the blackmailing. She knew what she was doing when she went out for those walks and left Sean alone with one or other of you.'

'Surely she murdered him,' said Angela.

144

'I would like to think that,' sighed Hamish. 'But at the time of the murder she was performing with a pop group in front of witnesses, and I cannae break her alibi. Keep quiet, all of you, and we might come out of this. But if I find one of you killed Sean Gourlay, then there will be no more covering anything up. I've got a week. In a week's time, Sean's mother comes up here to take away a few things and try to sell the bus. Of course, I could always put the video with the other things I found,' he added half to himself.

'You mean you found the missing drugs?' asked Angela eagerly.

'And the money?' put in Mrs Wellington.

'Yes.'

'Where?' asked Angela. 'Can't we have the money back, and the drugs?'

'No, I'm sorry. They'll have to stay where they are for now.'

When the women had gone, Hamish went through to the office and made notes, writing down what he knew, but without seeing any glimmer of hope.

The phone beside him rang. It was a tearful woman calling to say a truck had crashed into her car up on the moors. He drove off to deal with that but all the while his mind was turning over what he knew and worrying in case one of the three women was a murderess.

It was during that evening when the light began to fade and Willie was whistling to himself in the kitchen as he prepared the supper that Hamish, with a sudden lurch in his stomach, wondered if either of the three might go to the bus to try to find the money or drugs.

He shouted to Willie that he had to go out and to keep his dinner warm and made his way up to the manse field. The bus stood dark and forlorn. Hamish crouched down behind the packing case, deciding to give it an hour or so. Mrs Wellington and Angela, if they wanted to make a move, would do so before bedtime so as not to rouse their husbands' suspicions by getting up and going out in the middle of the night.

By eleven o'clock he was beginning to shiver, for the night was getting cold. He rose stiffly up from behind the packing case and then crouched down again. Three shadowy figures were at the edge of the field. He waited a moment and then switched on the large torch he was carrying, stood up and shone it straight at the bus. Angela, Mrs Wellington and Jessie Currie swung round and stood hypnotized in the light like startled rabbits.

Hamish walked towards them. Angela was carrying a hammer, no doubt to break the lock.

'I know what you're after,' said Hamish severely, 'and you're not getting it. Now, I'm going out on a limb and putting my job on the line for the lot of ye. The least you can all do iss not to try to tamper wi' the evidence more than it's been tampered with already. Off tae your beds, ladies, and if I see just one of you near this bus again I'll take the whole lot, video and all, and let Strathbane see it.'

They shuffled off silently, without a word.

Hamish followed them just as slowly. He was haunted by the sight of Angela holding that hammer. You think you know people so well, and when something like murder happens you realize you really don't know much about them at all. Angela had previously proved herself to be unstable, but the circumstances had been stressful. Mrs Wellington he had believed to be the sort of character of a Good Woman that she presented to the world, and Jessie and Nessie he had regarded affectionately as a couple of jokes. He must try Cheryl again.

Next morning, he told Willie he wanted the day off and asked him to look after things. Hamish cynically noticed his dog, who would normally have been scrabbling at the Land Rover, was happy to be left behind. Towser had been seduced by Willie's cooking.

He took Willie's battered Ford instead of the police car, not wanting to advertise his presence in Strathbane to anyone from head-quarters.

The farther he drove from Lochdubh, the more he felt like an irresponsible fool. He should never have become so involved with the locals in a murder inquiry. He should have phoned Strathbane, told them about the new evidence, and let them take it from there. For all he knew of them, Mrs Wellington, Angela, or even Jessie Currie might be capable of murder.

If only Cheryl hadn't so many witnesses. He would no doubt find her again and she would swear and curse and he would get nothing more out of her. He could not tell her about the video without risking exposing the three women.

It was all so hopeless.

He was approaching Mullen's Roadhouse. He slowed down. A large new poster was pinned up on the window. Top of the bill was Johnny Rankin and the Stotters. He stopped the car and climbed out. They were due to perform that evening.

He decided to phone Willie and say he would be in Strathbane until very late. He had to see that performance and judge if there was any way Cheryl might have managed to slip out. She had that scooter. But it would take about two hours surely to get to Lochdubh, park the scooter outside the village, go to the bus on foot, murder Sean, and then get back.

He was turning the problem over in his mind when a slim figure on a scooter shot past. Under the crash helmet he could see the driver had bright orange hair.

Cheryl!

He set off in pursuit, wishing he were in the Land Rover, wishing he could switch on the siren. The scooter had been painted bright pink and the licence plate was obscured by dirt, but there could not be more than one person in the Highlands with that colour of hair. The figure on the scooter glanced back and then simply swerved off the road on a forestry track and sped through the tall thin pine trees. Hamish swung the car off the road, but after only half a mile the track disappeared and ahead he could see that orange hair flitting off through the darkness of the trees.

He cursed under his breath, turned and went back to the road. He would go on to the campsite and confront Cheryl when she arrived.

When he drove into the campsite, that woman was still there, still stirring the pot. As he was not in a police car or in uniform, no one ran away at his arrival. There were fewer old buses and caravans this time, but the bright-blue one belonging to the Stoddarts was still there. He went up and knocked at the door. Again the thin bearded man answered it.

'I would like to wait until Cheryl Higgins returns, Mr Stoddart,' said Hamish.

'Why wait?' he asked amiably and then stood aside. 'Help yourself. Herself's in bed as usual.'

Chapter Eight

What will not woman, gentle woman dare,
When strong affection stirs her spirit up?
                              – Robert Southey

The Stoddarts were again watching television.
Hamish thought, as he leant over Cheryl to
wake her, that he would have expected the
Stoddarts to be weaving cloth, painting pictures or doing something artistic rather than
watching an Australian soap. They did not
seem in the least troubled by his presence.

Cheryl came awake, and as soon as she saw
who her visitor was, began her usual litany of
oaths and curses. Once he could get a word in,
Hamish asked, 'Where's your scooter?'

'Whit?'

'You heard.'

'I sold it,' she said sulkily.

'Who to?'

'Some fella I met in a bar.'

'What's his name?'

151

'I dinnae ken,' said Cheryl, shifting restlessly among the frowsty bedclothes. 'He gied me cash, I gied him the papers.'

'What did he look like?'

'Wee man wi' a leather jacket and black hair.'

'Why don't I believe you?' demanded Hamish plaintively. 'Were you out this morning?'

'No, I was here in ma bed.'

Hamish stood up and approached the Stoddarts. 'Was Cheryl out this morning?'

Wayne Stoddart wrenched his eyes from the television screen. 'Don't ask me, man,' he said. 'Only just got up.'

Bunty Stoddart, whose face was hidden under a tangled mass of hair, continued to watch and listen avidly to the Australian soap, a vision of sanitized life in the antipodean middle class.

Hamish returned to Cheryl. 'I think it was you I chased this morning. There can't be more than two of you in the Highlands with that colour of hair.'

Cheryl gave a contemptuous yawn.

Hamish gave up and went outside and began to search around for the scooter. The wind was howling through the piles of refuse and old cars which dotted the field among the buses and caravans. A dismal scene. But there was no sign of the scooter.

He began to experience a pressing nagging

fear that he was in the wrong place, that the clue to the murder lay back in Lochdubh, buried among the inhabitants. But he stubbornly decided to wait in Strathbane until evening and see Johnny Rankin and the Stotters. It was no use questioning Cheryl again. He would not get anything out of her.

He drove into Strathbane, a misery of a place with tall concrete blocks of flats and an air of failure. Nothing had changed. The sea-gulls here seemed dirtier than anywhere else and the oily sea sucked at the rubbish-strewn shore, heaving in on long rolling slow waves, as if exhausted by pollution. He went to the Glen Bar, which he had once frequented when he had been briefly stationed in the town, ordered an orange juice and then sat in a corner and took out a notebook and began to write anything that came into his head about the case.

It slowly dawned on him that he had let his feelings become involved in a dangerous way. Not only was he protecting the three women, he had not questioned Mr Ferrari thoroughly enough, having let his partiality for hard-working Scottish Italians sway his judgement. Then there was the minister. There was no doubt that the normally scholarly and gentle Mr Wellington had gone temporarily mad, and the murder had definitely been done by someone in the grip of a murderous rage. Had Mr

Wellington considered *himself* to be the hammer of God?

He had half a mind to call at headquarters and report the finding of the money, drugs and video and then ask for leave so that he could get away from the village and leave the Strathbane police to do their work.

But perhaps, just perhaps, he might find a clue during the performance of the pop group.

It was a long dreary day and he was glad when evening arrived and he drove to Mullen's Roadhouse, anxious to get it over with.

The huge bar was crowded with a mixture of young people wearing what looked to Hamish like an assortment of jogging suits, and staid Scottish couples who had no doubt come because the entertainment was free and there was nothing much else in the way of entertainment in Strathbane.

He was getting tired of orange juice and switched to tomato juice.

There was a small stage in the bar. Various young men were setting up sound equipment and plugging in things and arranging loud-speakers.

At last Johnny Rankin and the Stotters came on. Johnny Rankin was an emaciated young man wearing black leather trousers covered in sequins and nothing else. The only female performer was Cheryl, who was wearing an old-fashioned black corset and black stockings, perhaps hoping to emulate Madonna, although there was something peculiarly sexless about her, but then, reflected Hamish, he had always thought there was something peculiarly sexless about Madonna.

The band swung into action, a hellish cacophony of sound. Cheryl shouted the lyrics and gyrated and twanged a large electric guitar, making up in energy what she so obviously lacked in talent. Strobe lights hurt Hamish's eyes but he kept them fixed on Cheryl. At no time did she leave the stage. He suffered through the whole performance and then went out into the blessed quiet of the night, feeling low. There was no way Cheryl could have left the stage.

He drove back to Lochdubh, regretting that it was now too late to call on Priscilla – Priscilla who had a marvellous way of clarifying his thoughts. He resolved to see her the next day. The need to turn the evidence over to Strathbane was becoming pressing.

And then, as he was driving past the manse, he suddenly stopped abruptly a little beyond it and looked back up at the field. All the lights were on in the bus. He got out of the car and sprinted up towards the field.

He reached the bus and quietly leaned in through the door. Mr Wellington, the minister, was feverishly looking through the cupboards. Groceries and Sean's clothes were lying tumbled on the floor.

Hamish stepped inside.

'What the hell do you think you are doing?' he demanded.

Mr Wellington swung round, his face grey.

'I-I-I lent Sean a v-valuable book,' he stammered. 'I was looking for it.'

'In the middle of the night?' demanded Hamish. 'This iss breaking and entering.'

'I have a spare set of keys,' said Mr Wellington. 'Sean left them at the manse in case he should ever lose his own.'

'Then it wass your job to turn them over to the police,' snapped Hamish, torn between anxiety and fear. 'Do you know what I think? I think you either killed Sean yourself or you think your wife did it.'

The minister began to slowly replace everything in the cupboard without speaking.

'I will need to report this,' said Hamish heavily.

The minister sat down suddenly on a bench seat at the table and buried his face in his hands. Hamish sat on the bench opposite him. 'Tell me what you know,' he said gently, 'and I will see what I can do to help.'

'He was an evil man,' muttered the minister. 'I thought when he was dead that everything would return to normal. But my wife is still a wreck.' He took his hands from his face and looked at Hamish and then gave an odd little sob like a tired child. 'You may as well charge me and get it over with, Hamish. I killed him.'

Hamish felt deathly tired.

'How?' he asked.

'I took the sledge-hammer and hit him.'

'Where?'

'Right here ... in the bus.'

'I don't mean that. I mean, where did you strike him?'

The minister looked at him and then said slowly, 'I waited until he had his back to me and then I brought the hammer down on the back of his head.'

Hamish felt a wave of relief. 'Mr Wellington, you did not see the body or hear the pathologist's report. The blow that killed him was the very first one and that was a blow to the forehead. Once he was down, the murderer kept on hitting until his head and face were wrecked.'

'Yes, yes, that was it,' said Mr Wellington eagerly. 'I had forgotten.'

'Havers,' said Hamish. 'You didn't forget because you didn't do it, but you thought your wife did. Why?'

The minister looked defiantly at Hamish and then seemed to collapse. 'She was in his bus on the night of the murder,' he said.

'What!'

'It was right after the evening service. I saw her walk across. I followed her. I couldn't hear what she was saying but she was crying when she came out. I seized her and demanded to know what was wrong. She became almost hysterical and refused to tell me. I took her indoors and went back. Sean laughed at me and said she had lost her faith as well and was pleading with him to hand it back, just like a book, he said. I tried to punch him, but he was so very strong. He simply picked me up and threw me out on to the grass, laughing his head off.

'I told my wife what he had said and she agreed that was the case. I suggested we pray together and then she began to laugh at me in a terrible parody of Sean's laughter and told me not to be such an old fool. Later that evening, I heard the back door slam and was sure she had gone back to him again. Perhaps Sean was in love with her. Mrs Wellington can be a very seductive woman, although she is not aware of it.'

Hamish thought of the large and tweedy Mrs Wellington and blinked.

'Your wife has not been honest with me,' he said. 'Look, put all the stuff away, lock up and give me the keys. Get your wife out of bed.'

But by the time everything was put away, Hamish had decided to leave interviewing Mrs Wellington until the morning. He said he

would call for her and take her along to the
police station. If he interviewed her now, he
would find it hard to get her alone without the
minister. Although his loyalty to the three
blackmailed women had been badly shaken,
he still did not want to speak to her in front of
her husband and so reveal to the minister that
his wife was a thief.

Willie was asleep in his room by the time
Hamish got home. He went to bed but did not
undress. He lay on top of it, with Towser at
his feet, worrying. Evidence was piling on
evidence and he was keeping it all from
Strathbane.

He fell into a heavy sleep at dawn and
awoke at nine o'clock, all the worries pouring
back into his brain. His one thought was to
see Priscilla before he interviewed Mrs
Wellington.

'You cannae go out like that,' said Willie
reprovingly from the kitchen sink. 'You've no'
shaved and you look as if you've slept in your
clothes.'

'Haven't time,' said Hamish. 'Look after
Towser for me.'

He drove up to the castle. Priscilla was in the
office, working at the computer.

'Hamish! What has happened?' she cried.
'You look awful.'

The door of the office opened and her father
came in and bristled at the sight of Hamish.

'Shouldn't you be about your duties, officer?' he barked. 'I don't want you coming in here and keeping my daughter from her work.'

'I've nearly finished,' said Priscilla. 'Go away, Daddy.'

'Show a bit of respect for your father,' raged the colonel. 'You used to be such a sweet child and you've changed since you came under the pernicious influence of this layabout.'

He stormed out.

'Rats,' said Priscilla, switching off the computer. 'Now he'll be in a foul mood all day. You smell awful, Hamish. Have you started smoking again?'

'No, I was at Mullen's bar last night, and there was enough smoke in there to make an old-fashioned London fog.'

'Of course, some normal people change their clothes from day to day,' said Priscilla sweetly. 'You'd best come upstairs to my quarters, Hamish, or Daddy will be back to make trouble.'

She led him up to the top of the castle, where she had turned two servants' rooms into a bedroom and sitting room for herself.

Hamish looked around appreciatively. The small room was bright with chintz and flowers and the windows were open to let in the heavy, warm air blowing in off the Gulf Stream. He settled down and told her everything that had happened.

'You are in a mess,' commented Priscilla.

'Do you think I should tell Strathbane?'

'My common sense tells me you should tell them everything as quickly as possible, my emotions tell me to keep it all quiet for a bit longer. You're going to have to start questioning everyone all over again. Do you remember when Sean was popular in the village? And then, when he was killed, no one had a good word to say for him? Look at it this way. I think he only directly affected the Curries, the Wellingtons, Cheryl and Angela. But sooner or later that odd sort of Highland telepathy in this village beamed in on the nastiness of the real Sean. Besides, they're quite happy to tolerate some layabout on the dole. They don't like it when the layabout seems to have money to throw around the place on gifts from this shop and meals at the Napoli. So if any man or woman had been up at that bus on the night of the murder as well as Mrs Wellington, who's going to tell you? Your suspects are desperate to have the murder solved in the hope that their own activities might be covered up, but the villagers would protect one of their own, even if they suspected that person of murder. Mrs Wellington was at the bus. Maybe *she* saw someone else that evening.'

Hamish passed a weary hand over his unshaven face. 'You're right. I'd better go.'

'Wait and have some coffee and I'll go and borrow an electric razor for you. You've got red bristles.'

When she handed him a mug of coffee, Hamish looked at the television set and video in the corner and then at the various remote controls on the table. 'I thought you only needed one control,' he said, picking one of them up.

'We've got satellite TV now,' said Priscilla. 'I'll leave you to play with it while I get you that razor. Press 5 on this one and that'll get you satellite TV and then press the various channels on this other one.'

Hamish idly switched through the channels, finally ending up with a music one. A thin girl was gyrating to a thudding beat. She was wearing a brief black leather bikini and thigh-length leather boots. 'All I gotta say is, screw you, baby,' she sang.

'Is that supposed to be sexy?' Hamish asked Priscilla as she came in and handed him a razor.

'Not to you,' laughed Priscilla. 'That's Jonathan Carty.'

'Are you telling me that's a bloke?'

'Yes, a transvestite.'

'But he's got boobs!'

'Silicone injections, Hamish. The marvels of modern science.'

'Tcha.' He switched it off.

162

'Don't worry, Hamish. The moral revolution's coming. Reaction will set in and even mild womanizers like yourself will be regarded as evil beasts.'

'I am not the womanizer,' said Hamish. 'Where's the bathroom?'

'Along the corridor and on your left. Have a bath while you're at it. I left one of Daddy's clean shirts on the chair in there for you.'

'He'll kill you!'

'I really don't take any notice of his rages any more,' said Priscilla. 'If someone's always raging about something or another, one ceases to listen.'

Hamish bathed and shaved and felt considerably better. He said goodbye to Priscilla and drove to the manse and collected Mrs Wellington despite protests from the minister. Instead of going to the police station, he drove up on the moors and parked off the road on a heathery track.

'Willie's at the station,' he said, 'and I'm still trying to protect you, but I don't know how long I can go on doing it. I want the whole truth and nothing but the truth. Now, you were at the bus on the night of the murder. When exactly?'

'Nine o'clock,' she said in a dull voice.

'Why did you go?'

'I pleaded with him to give me that video. He asked for a thousand pounds. I began to cry. I begged him. I said I could not possibly get that amount of money and he . . . he laughed at me. I was only there for a few minutes. I realized it was hopeless, so I left. My husband grabbed me outside. He demanded to know what I had been saying, why I had been there, but I could not tell him. Then he returned to the manse later and said Sean had told him I was worried about losing my faith. For one wild moment I felt hope. Sean had not betrayed me. Perhaps he would relent. And then I realized that of course he would not tell my husband the truth while there was still hope of getting money out of me for his silence.'

'And you went back out again? Where? Back to the bus?'

Mrs Wellington hung her head. 'I couldn't go back. There were men there.'

'Men!' Hamish howled in exasperation. 'What men?'

'Mr Ferrari from the restaurant and two others.'

'Good God, woman,' raged Hamish, 'why did you not tell me this before?'

She raised her head and glared at him with something of her old manner and said distinctly, 'Because if they killed him, I was not going to betray them for doing a service for mankind!'

Hamish forced himself to be calm with an effort. 'So where did you go?'

'Down on the beach. I walked for a long time, a very long time. I thought of walking into the water and putting an end to the misery, but I could not even find the courage to do that.'

'Look,' said Hamish urgently, 'Mr Wellington's a Christian minister of the church. It is his duty to forgive. Why don't you tell him?'

'No man is a Christian when it comes to his own wife,' she said. 'I can't.'

'You may have to,' warned Hamish. 'I'd best see Mr Ferrari . . . and you had better start saying your prayers again.'

Half an hour later, Hamish was sitting opposite Mr Ferrari in the flat above the restaurant. It always amazed him that a man who looked so Italian could have such a strong Scottish accent.

'Well, Mr Ferrari,' began Hamish, 'I have it on good authority that yourself and two men were up at that bus on the night of the murder.' Mr Ferrari went as still as a lizard on a rock when a shadow crosses it. His old unblinking eyes surveyed Hamish from among the network of brown wrinkles on his face. 'I guess the other two men were Luigi and Giovanni,' said Hamish.

'That is so,' said Mr Ferrari. He took a small black cheroot out of a box on a table next to him and lit it carefully.

'Why did you not tell me?' demanded Hamish.

'Because none of us committed murder, therefore the purpose of our visit was irrelevant,' said Mr Ferrari, blowing a perfect smoke ring in Hamish's direction.

'Anything that happened on the night of the murder is relevant,' said Hamish. 'Either tell me here or come to the station with me and make a statement.'

There was a long silence. Then Mr Ferrari said, 'I have come to love this village. I am part of it. I am involved in the welfare of Lochdubh. Sean Gourlay in the eyes of the villagers had outstayed his welcome. It was evident to all that he was the reason for Mrs Wellington's distress, although no one knew why. I took it upon myself to tell him to move on.'

'With threats?'

'Dinnae be daft,' he said, his accent broadening. 'I told him if he stayed on I would see to it that the shops did not serve him.'

'And what did he say to that?'

'He said he would move.'

Hamish leaned back in his chair and momentarily closed his eyes. He was in no doubt that Mr Ferrari had threatened Sean with physical violence. Perhaps he had carried out that threat.

'I will type up a statement,' said Hamish, 'and get you to sign it. I will also have to take statements from Luigi and Giovanni.'

Mr Ferrari carefully stubbed out his cheroot. He looked thoughtfully at Hamish from under heavy-lidded eyes. 'I am not pleased that you are pursuing inquiries into the death of a piece of shit,' he said evenly. 'I am not pleased with you at all, Sergeant.'

'Listen to me, Mr Ferrari,' said Hamish, standing up, 'this is not Italy. There are no headmen in this village, and I for one will not tolerate anyone who tries to achieve his ends with threats. You are not pleased with me! Just who the hell do you think you are?'

Hamish stalked back to the station and typed up the statement. He took it back and waited until Mr Ferrari signed it and then took statements from Luigi and Giovanni.

At five o'clock, Luigi and Giovanni called at the police station. With many smiles and deprecatory waves of the hands they said they had come to collect Mr Ferrari's television set, which had been 'on loan'.

'You must hae done something to make them mad,' said Willie after they had left, carrying the set between them. 'Och, jist when I thought I might have a chance wi' Lucia.'

'You've got a snowball's chance in hell,' said Hamish with true Highland malice. 'The only thing that's likely to marry you, Willie Lamont, is a vacuum cleaner.'

'Fat lot you know, *sir*,' said Willie. 'Thon Lucia's a *real* woman.' And he wrenched off his apron, dragged on his coat and went out and slammed the door.

Hamish slumped down in his favourite armchair, tossed his cap on the floor and stretched out his long legs. He thought of the Curries, of Angela Brodie, of Mrs Wellington and groaned. 'Damn all women,' he said and closed his eyes and fell fast asleep.

He plunged straight into a dream in which he had just got married to Priscilla and they were on their honeymoon. They were in a hotel bedroom and Priscilla was undressing and he was staring in horror at her flat, muscled, hairy chest. 'What's the matter, Hamish?' laughed Priscilla. 'Didn't you know I was a man?'

He woke up sweating and stared sightlessly across the room, his heart pounding. What a nightmare! It must have been because of the awful day and because of that transvestite he had seen on television.

And then he sat up straight. When he had woken Cheryl yesterday morning, she had been groggy with sleep and she had been wearing a dirty old night-gown. How could she have fled from him on a scooter one minute and been in bed the next? The route the figure on the scooter had taken through the trees had been *away* from the direction of the campsite.

He dived through to the office and phoned Strathbane and asked to speak to Jimmy Anderson. 'Whit now?' demanded Jimmy.

'Look,' said Hamish, 'this may be a daft question, but among the so-called pop singers in Strathbane, is there one who dresses as a woman?'

'A transvestite like?'

'Aye, wi' orange hair, slim, maybe girlish-looking.'

'There's the one wi' black hair, or had the last time I saw him.'

'Name?'

'Real name I dinnae ken, for he hisnae been in trouble with us. Time was when we could hae banged him up for dressing like a lassie, but them were the good auld days.'

'Name?' shouted Hamish.

'Bert Luscious, would you believe.'

'Where . . . where does he live?'

'I don't know. But he does a turn at a drag club doon by the docks called Jessie's.'

'A drag club in *Strathbane*!'

'We move wi' the times, Hamish, laddie, we move wi' the times. Started up a few months ago. Put a plainclothes man in for a few nights, but he said it was all quiet, no drugs, no may-hem, jist a lot of fellows in lassies' frocks.'

'Thanks,' said Hamish feverishly.

'Whit fur? Are ye intae the marabou and rhinestones yourself?'

'Maybe,' said Hamish and put down the phone. He scrabbled in his desk and came up with a notebook he had used when Sean and Cheryl had appeared on that scooter. He had taken the number. But if she had sold it, he could not find out the new owner until morn-ing. Damn. He should have phoned immedi-ately after he got back.

He went to the Napoli restaurant. Willie was sitting comfortably at a corner table being waited on by Lucia. 'I'm off again,' said Hamish curtly. 'You'd best get back to the station in case any urgent calls come through.'

Lucia looked at Hamish as if he were a monster. Then, 'Go along,' she said quietly to Willie. 'Giovanni will bring your meal and your wine over to you.'

As Hamish left, Mr Ferrari held open the door for him. His thin purplish lips were parted in a smile which did not reach his eyes.

Chapter Nine

When gloamin' treads the heels o' day
And birds sit courin' on the spray,
Alang the flower'y hedge I stray,
To meet my ain dear somebody.
                    – Robert Tannahill

Hamish took Towser with him, frightened that a lovelorn Willie would neglect the dog. He put the dog's blanket and water bowl in the back of the Land Rover, along with a helping of cold pasta he had found in the kitchen.

As he once more took the long road to Strathbane, he wondered that a drag club could survive anywhere in the Highlands. 'Jessie' was the Scottish word for an effeminate man, a shortened version of the old English sneer of jessamy. No doubt that was why the place was called Jessie's. He did not want to advertise to the customers that he was a policeman, but neither did he want to borrow a frock from Priscilla and dress up. He was not in uniform but in a dark-blue sweater, checked shirt and dark-blue cords. He could only hope that some of the other customers were similarly attired.

He found Jessie's on the waterfront in Strathbane, housed in what used to be a ship's chandler's. Music was thudding out into the acrid air of Strathbane. He locked the Land Rover after filling Towser's water and food bowls and made his way inside, blinking to accustom his eyes to the darkness.

To his relief, the customers were practically all in conventional dress and included some obviously staid married couples who had simply come to see the show. In order to get in, he had had to pay the club membership of five pounds. He was ushered to a table in a corner by a young man dressed unimaginatively in striped T-shirt and skin-tight black trousers who served him orange juice and charged him two pounds for it.

On the stage someone in low-cut gown and sequins and feathered headdress was belting out 'Hello, Dolly'. He was obviously the star turn, looking like a glamorous woman compared to the sequinned chorus who looked what they probably were, small Scotsmen with bad legs. As the show went on, Hamish was able to understand the club's obvious popularity with a respectable section of the population because it mostly consisted of popular numbers from musicals, all quite well staged and mostly well sung. But there was no sign of Bert Luscious.

He signalled to the waiter, told him he was a policeman, and asked to see the owner. After about fifteen minutes, the waiter returned and asked Hamish to follow him to 'the back o' the house'.

He pushed open a door and said, 'Jessie'll see you now,' and Hamish went in.

Jessie turned out to be the man who had sung 'Hello, Dolly'. He was still in costume but had removed his blond wig to reveal a shaven head. The small room was made up like a star's dressing room in miniature with lights around the mirror and a Victorian chaise longue in one corner.

'What iss up?' demanded Jessie in an accent that Hamish guessed probably hailed from South Uist in the Outer Hebrides, having a soft, whistling sort of sibilancy.

'Nothing up with the club,' said Hamish. 'I'm looking for someone called Bert Luscious.'

'Not on tonight, precious.'

'Can you give me his address?'

'And why should I be doing that, officer?'

'Because I am on a murder inquiry and it is your duty to help the police.'

Jessie sighed and then pulled a large book towards him, scattering sticks of grease-paint as he did so. With one large white well-shaped hand, he flicked through the pages. 'Aye, here we are. Quite close by, he is. Number 141, Highland Towers, on the estate up back.'

'Thanks,' said Hamish.

Jessie batted his false eyelashes at him. 'Enjoy the show, sweetie?'

'Yes,' said Hamish awkwardly, backing towards the door. 'Why Jessie?' he asked.

'Because that's what all those nasty little boys at school used to call me – Big Jessie. My real name is Cyril Crumb, and believe me, anything iss better than that.'

As Hamish drove towards the tower blocks which overlooked the waterfront, he reflected dismally that he could hardly claim this night's expenses, as he was not even supposed to be in Strathbane.

Bert Luscious's flat was on the sixth floor but the urine-stinking lift was out of order and so he had to trudge up the stairs and then along a gallery which led outside the flats, listening to the sounds of drunken quarrels, crying babies and television sets coming through the thin walls.

Number 141 was in darkness but he could hear the blast of a stereo coming from inside, thumping out rap. He rang the bell. No answer. He thudded on the door and waited but no one came to answer it. He tried the handle and the door swung open.

A fetid, sweet smell met his nostrils and he groped about the minuscule hallway until he found the light switch. A joss-stick was burning in a milk bottle on a table, hence the smell. The noise of music was coming from behind a door to his right. He opened it.

He found himself looking into a living room, cluttered and messy with dirty clothes strewn about the battered furniture. On a sideboard a large ghettoblaster shattered the air with sound. He crossed the room and switched it off.

Next door a television set mumbled on through the walls, punctuated with an occasional burst of canned laughter. 'Anybody home?' he called.

He walked back into the hallway and tried the door opposite. This proved to be a squalid bedroom: unmade bed, dirty stained sheets, posters on the walls of singers with guitars.

He left that and tried the bathroom and then walked into a small kitchen at the back of the hall.

Bert Luscious was seated at the kitchen table, his long orange hair spilling out over a cheap plastic top. Hamish tried to rouse him and then saw the syringe lying beside his head, half covered by his hair. He felt his limp wrist. There was only a flutter of a pulse.

Hamish swore under his breath. It looked as if Bert had taken an overdose. He, Hamish,

would have to explain his presence in Strathbane, for he would need to get Bert to the
nearest hospital.

He found a telephone buried under a pile of
clothes on the living room floor and phoned
for an ambulance, and then with great reluc-
tance phoned Strathbane Police Headquarters.
He asked to be put through to Jimmy
Anderson, briefly told him what he had found
and said he hoped it could somehow be kept
from Blair at the moment.

'Everything can be kept from Blair at the
moment,' said Anderson cheerfully. 'He's in
the hospital wi' cirrhosis o' the liver. Be round
right away.'

Hamish began to search feverishly after
drawing on a thin pair of gloves which he always kept on him for examining clues without
leaving his own fingerprints on them. He found
the papers which showed that Bert was now the
owner of Cheryl's scooter. He found some
photographs of Bert in action and was startled
at the young man's resemblance to Cheryl.

Then, feeling like a criminal, he carefully put
everything back where he had found it, knowing full well that he was not supposed to touch
anything before the CID arrived. He had just
finished when he heard the approaching wail
of the ambulance and police cars.

Hamish explained to Jimmy Anderson that
he had just heard that Bert had orange hair

and performed as a woman and had wondered whether that might have been the way
Cheryl could have been at Lochdubh murder-
ing Sean when she was supposed to be on
stage. But he said nothing of his find of the
money and drugs, nor of the blackmailing of
the women. For a mad idea had taken root in
his brain, an idea that might flush out the
murderer with the least scandal possible.

But he patiently went back to headquarters
with Anderson and typed up a statement. The
report from the hospital said Bert was in a very
bad way and no one would be able to interview him for some time.

Hamish then drove out to Mullen's Roadhouse. Sure enough, Johnny Rankin and the
Stotters were gyrating and howling to the end
of their performance. Cheryl gave him a filthy
look as she finally climbed down from the
stage.

'Don't worry,' said Hamish. 'I'm not here to
ask you any more questions. Did you collect
all your belongings from the bus?'

'Yes.'

'Well, I'm glad of that, for Sean's mother is
coming up the day after tomorrow to take
away her son's things. But before she touches
anything, the forensic team is coming back
because I have found some items for them that
they missed before and that I am sure will give

us definite proof of the murderer. I swear they're covered in fingerprints.'

Cheryl shrugged and her hair fell forward to hide her face. 'When's this forensic lot coming?' she asked.

'Let me see, this is Wednesday ... no, it's Thursday already, so that means Friday morning I'm expecting them.'

'Oh, aye.' Cheryl turned away, indifference in every line of her body.

But it must work. It's got to work, thought Hamish as he drove home. I'll tell the Wellingtons, the Curries, and Angela Brodie, and Mr Ferrari, too, that I've found stuff which will enable the forensic department to find the murderer. Forensic investigation is the new witchcraft. Any guilty person's going to be frightened of being smelt out.

And if it doesn't work, reflected Hamish sadly, I'll turn everything over to Strathbane and throw myself on Jimmy Anderson's mercy. What a gamble! What a thin chance! But the murderer, or murderess, must be badly frightened, must still be desperate to cover his or her tracks. And if I get whoever did it, then I have to gamble on that person keeping quiet about the blackmailing. If it's Cheryl, point out that she'll get a more lenient sentence; if it's Ferrari, he didn't know about the blackmailing anyway. But if it's one of the others, the blackmailing is their best excuse for the murder and whoever it is will damn the other two innocent blackmail victims when presenting her defence. But it can't go on. I'll have to try.

The next day, he decided that there must have been something in the orange juice he had bought at the club. He was behaving ridiculously. Better to wait until Bert recovered from his drug overdose and get Jimmy Anderson to find out if he had stood in for Cheryl on the night of the murder. Then question Johnny Rankin and the rest. Then see if Cheryl could be broken. It was possible she did not know of the blackmailing, but how could she not know? But something drove him on to get Mrs Wellington, Jessie Currie and Angela Brodie on their own and tell them a variety of what he had told Cheryl. All looked at him hopelessly, as if they were exhausted with weeping and worry.

When Hamish returned to the police station, Willie said, 'Jimmy Anderson was on the phone. You're to call right back.'

Hamish phoned Strathbane and was put through to the detective. 'It's Bert Luscious, real name Bert Maxwell,' said Anderson. 'He's been and gone and died on us. I had a go at Johnny Rankin and the rest and they swear blind Cheryl was with them all the time and I cannae break their story. Rankin's got enough syringe marks on his arms tae make him look like a walking pincushion, but he started screaming about police harassment and said he's been clean for months. We searched his flat and the others but couldnae find any drugs. Look, Hamish, Mullen tells me you've been tae the Roadhouse and it's no' on your beat. You're going tae have to look the facts in the face, and it's that one o' that lot in Brigadoon up there did it, and stop running yourself ragged wi' a bunch o' daft men in women's frocks and a lot o' drug addicts who can't sing for two pence. Are you keeping anything back?'

Hamish said reluctantly, 'I've got new evidence. Mrs Wellington, the minister's wife, was back at the bus on the night of the murder, so was her husband, and so was the restaurant owner, Ferrari, and a couple of his relatives.'

'And why havenae we seen those statements?'

'I've just done them,' said Hamish.

'Look here, when is that mother coming up tae sell the bus?'

'In a few days' time.'

'Well, I'm coming up there tomorrow to go over the whole thing again, and do you know why, Hamish Macbeth?'

'No.'

'Because I've got a feeling in ma bones you're protecting someone. If Blair's as bad as

180

I think he is, he'll have to retire and I'm in line for promotion, so it's no more easygoing auld Jimmy Anderson. See you in the morn.'

Priscilla, thought Hamish. I need Priscilla, and as if on cue, Priscilla walked into the office.

'Sit down,' said Hamish. 'I'm in a grand old mess.'

Willie came in with a tray of coffee. 'Willie, could you take off your pinny and go on your beat,' said Hamish. 'We want to be alone.'

'Why?'

'Use your brains, man, I've got something serious to ask Miss Halburton-Smythe.'

'Oh, I see,' said Willie. 'I'll give you a long time then.'

When Willie had gone, Hamish outlined what had happened to date and his plans for catching the murderer.

'It might just work,' said Priscilla. 'What will you do if no one turns up?'

'I'll chust haff to tell Anderson everything.'

'I suppose you can lie and tell him you just found the stuff. When do you expect your murderer to show?'

'After dark.'

'That'll be about midnight, and even then it never gets really dark at this time of year,' pointed out Priscilla. 'If I were you, I would begin watching about ten. I've got a nifty little tape recorder up at the castle. I'll bring that and keep you company.'

'Nice of you, but why?'

'Better to have proof and a witness.'

'And what do I tell Willie?' asked Hamish.

'Tell him we're walking out. He thinks you're proposing to me anyway.'

'Och, no,' said Hamish. 'The man can't be that daft.'

'I'm telling you for a fact,' said PC Willie Lamont in Patel's grocery store, 'that Hamish Macbeth is in that polis station right now proposing marriage to Priscilla Halburton-Smythe.'

'High time,' said Mrs Maclean.

'Our Hamish getting married!' Mr Patel's dark face lit up. He enjoyed a good bit of gossip. 'Well, I never thought to see the day. My, my, my. And it's yourself, Mrs Anderson, and how are you this fine day? Have you heard the news about our Hamish?'

A reporter from the *Strathbane and Highland Gazette*, who was standing patiently behind Mrs Anderson waiting to buy a packet of cigarettes, pricked up his ears. Nice gossip piece. Forget the cigarettes. He'd better phone it over right away.

Hamish and Priscilla made their way to the field behind the manse by a circuitous route so that they would not be seen. This involved walking all the way over to Gunn's farm and then doubling back over the fields, past the greenish water-filled quarry and then up the steep path by the side of a cliff which overlooked the water, and so down towards the manse.

The twilight, or gloaming, as it is called in Scotland, was soft and clear. The residents of Lochdubh went early to bed, and as Hamish and Priscilla sat down in the field behind the shelter of the bus, the lights in the village were going out one by one.

They sat talking quietly of this and that but gradually fell silent, straining their ears for the slightest sound.

By one o'clock, the wind of Sutherland had risen and was moaning through the long grass and gaining in force every minute, filling the night with movement.

'We'll never hear anything in this,' whispered Priscilla.

'I'm a fool,' muttered Hamish bitterly. 'These damn women should never have put themselves in a position to be blackmailed anyway, and they'd better face up and take their medicine. Why should I protect them and risk letting a murderer go free?'

'Because Sean was a worthless man and these women are not worthless. They just did not have any experience of evil before. They were all so innocent and he took advantage of that.'

'Aye, I've had bad dreams over this. I had one about you, Priscilla.'

'Oh, what was I doing?'

'We were on our honeymoon and you were taking off your clothes and you had a flat hairy chest.'

'You know how to flatter a girl and make her feel good, Hamish.'

'It wass chust a dream! You do not haff the flat hairy chest!'

'How do you know?' said Priscilla huffily.

'Because . . .' He grabbed her by the arms in a fierce grip. 'Listen!' he muttered.

'Only the wind,' whispered Priscilla

'I don't *hear* anything exactly. I feel something coming.'

'"By the pricking of my thumbs, something wicked this way . . ."'

'Shhh!' He put a hand over her mouth.

Priscilla eased away from him and brought out the little tape recorder, switched it on and handed it to him.

Hamish stiffened like a hunting dog. His whole attention was focused on the packing case, whose light-brown sides glimmered faintly in the half-dark.

Then he let out a long 'aaaah' of satisfaction.

'Stay here,' he whispered. He walked slowly to where the bent figure was tearing the rocks out of the packing case.

'Cheryl Higgins,' he said. 'I charge you with

the murder of Sean Gourlay.' He shone a powerful torch full in her face.

'You're daft,' she snarled. 'Sean was hiding something here and he'd taken some o' ma things, and I remembered he might hae put them here.'

So, thought Hamish bleakly, she could well stick to that story and look horrified and surprised when the contents of that bag were revealed.

He looked at her in sudden hatred and the lie sprang easily to his lips. 'It won't do, Cheryl,' he said. 'Bert Luscious spoke before he died. He said he'd stood in for you on the night of the murder.' And with the inspiration of the desperate, Hamish added, 'and you promised him that scooter of yours if he did it.'

She backed away from him, a slight figure in black leather, her long hair whipped this way and that by the wind. 'You'll never get me in prison,' she said viciously. 'Not for that bastard. I told Sean I wus pregnant and he said, "Here's money. Get rid of it." I kep' the money and got it done on the National Health. Bastard.'

'So you killed him,' said Hamish.

'I didnae mean tae,' she said, sounding suddenly weary. 'I came back to see him. Johnny and the others said they would keep quiet. Sean loved me once. I drove the scooter from

Strathbane and left it up on the moors and crept down into the village. There were some men at the bus and I waited, lying in the grass until they went away. Then I went in. Sean had got the sledge-hammer because he said there was a gale blowing up and he was going tae put ropes ower the bus. I picked up the sledge. "Going to help me?" he said with that laugh, the way he had laughed when he told me to get rid of the baby. Oh, God, he'd said he loved me and would always look after me.' Her voice broke on a sob. 'So I smashed him and smashed him until there was nothing left that would attract a woman again.'

'What is here,' asked Hamish, 'that would incriminate you and not in the bus?'

'You didnae know,' she marvelled. 'You set me up and I fell for it. I hid the money and drugs for him and my fingerprints are all ower the stuff. And you didnae know. You're a bastard! I thought once you got my fingerprints on the stuff, you'd never leave me be. And I wanted the money and I wanted that video from the bus he was blackmailing those village women with. I was going to make them suffer.'

Hamish stepped forward. 'If you will accompany me to the police station, I –'

'NO!' she howled, a great scream which rose above the wind.

She whipped around and set out over the field like a deer. Hamish sprinted after her, caught his foot in a rabbit hole and went sprawling. Cursing, he got to his feet and ran on, deaf to Priscilla's cries behind him. The moon had risen and he could make out Cheryl's slight figure as it flew across the fields towards the quarry. As he pounded after her, he suddenly wondered if she knew about the quarry, she had always gone for walks around the village, and stopped, cupped his hands to his mouth and shouted a warning.

But she went straight on, straight to the edge and straight over.

Panting, he ran up and knelt down at the edge of the cliff over the quarry. The moon was shining on the spreading ripples on the water.

He hurtled down the bank at the side to where the waters of the old quarry were on a level with the ground, kicked off his shoes, laid the tape recorder on the shore and waded in. He dived and dived, groping desperately among the tentacles of the slimy weed which covered the bottom. From above the quarry came the sounds of voices.

He was nearing the end of his strength when his searching hands located a body tied tightly in the embrace of the weed. He surfaced, gulped air and dived once more, this time with his clasp-knife in his hand. He cut the body free and dragged it to the surface.

A little group of villagers, who had been alerted by Priscilla's cries for help, stood silently huddled together on the beach. He laid Cheryl down. Dr Brodie came hurrying up as Hamish was trying to revive the girl and pushed him aside. He felt Cheryl's pulse and then slowly shook his head.

'She's dead, Hamish. Nothing can be done for her now.'

Ian Gunn, the farmer, drove up in his old rusty Land Rover. Cheryl's body was lifted into the back and the doors slammed on it. 'Take it to the surgery and the ambulance from Strathbane will collect it,' said Dr Brodie. Ian nodded, climbed into the driving seat and drove slowly off, but the field was bumpy and he hit a rock and Cheryl's body jerked up in the back of the Land Rover, and for one horrible moment her white face, lit up by the moonlight, stared back at the watchers through the back windows.

Hamish gave a shiver. 'We should have closed her eyes,' he said wearily. 'Why did we forget to close her eyes?'

Dawn was breaking. Hamish had changed into dry clothes. Detectives Jimmy Anderson and Harry MacNab were sitting in his living room facing him. Priscilla sat beside Hamish on the sofa. In his bedroom, Willie slept on, as he had slept during the whole business.

'So, Hamish,' said Anderson, 'you've got it

sewn up nicely. And you've got her confession on tape! Good man. Where is it?'

'It iss where I left it,' said Hamish slowly. 'It iss by the old quarry.'

'No, it's not,' said Priscilla cheerfully. 'I picked it up.' She opened her handbag and drew out the tape recorder.

Hamish gave her an agonized look. On that tape was Cheryl's voice not only admitting to the murder but talking about the drugs and money and the video. 'Chust leave it be, Priscilla,' he said quickly. 'I'll type it up, Jimmy, and let you have it.'

'No, let's hear it now,' said Anderson. 'How does it work? I was never any good wi' gadgets.'

'Simple,' said Priscilla, seemingly oblivious to Hamish's warning look. 'You just press this button here.'

Hamish covered his face with his hands as Cheryl's voice sounded into the room. The tape ran on to the bit about Cheryl confessing to smashing Sean and then there was Hamish's voice saying she should accompany him to the police station and Cheryl shouting 'No!' and then nothing but the sound of Hamish running and panting and then his shouting a warning about the quarry.

Hamish slowly took his hands down from his face. Priscilla was sitting there calmly, as cool as a lettuce in a tailored green dress. The whole piece about the drugs, the money and the video had miraculously disappeared from the tape.

'Well, I must say you did a grand job, Sergeant,' said Anderson. Hamish glanced at him. Could it be his imagination, or had Anderson become more pompous in manner and heavier in figure? Was the mantle of the repulsive Blair about to fall on his shoulders? 'Of course,' went on Anderson, 'I consider it my duty to put in my report that the case could've maybe been solved earlier if you had not decided to investigate the Strathbane end on your own.'

'That's unfair,' said Priscilla.

'A good detective is always honest in his report,' said Anderson.

The telephone rang in the police station and Hamish went through to answer it.

'When I'm Detective Chief Inspector, Mac-Nab,' said Anderson, 'I'll be keeping Macbeth up to the mark. So he tricked that girl into a confession, but it's most irregular.'

Hamish came in with a smile on his face. 'I've got the grand news,' he said. 'That was Turnbull from Strathbane. He forgot to tell you last night that Blair is recovering. He'll soon be back on the job.'

Anderson seemed to dwindle in size to his former thin shape. 'Pillock!' he said. 'Here, Hamish, hae you any whisky?'

'A good copper does not drink on duty,' said Hamish primly.

'Come on, Hamish, I'm off duty as from now.'

'Particularly,' went on Hamish, 'a good copper who plans to put in a bad report about me.'

'Did I say that?' Anderson looked wounded. 'There'll be nothing but praise.'

'In that case,' said Hamish, 'I seem to mind I have the bottle somewhere.'

Chapter Ten

*'Mid pleasures and palaces though we may roam,
Be it ever so humble, there's no place like home.*
— John Howard Payne

Anderson and MacNab had finally left, Cheryl's body had been taken to Strathbane, and Hamish, supplied with black coffee by Priscilla, had typed up his report.

He came back into the living room and sat down with a sigh. 'What a night! Now, tell me how on earth you managed to doctor that tape.'

'Easy. The minute I heard Cheryl was dead, I ran back to the castle with it. Someone had found it on the shore and I grabbed it and said I'd give it to you. I simply cut that bit out of the tape and then spliced it together again.'

'How did you know how to do that?'

'Oh, some friend showed me how some time ago. You'd better get to bed, Hamish.'

'Not yet. I've got to get that stuff up from

193

under the packing case and I've got to erase the video. Are you awfully tired, or can you get the three women here?'

'Yes, but what about Willie?'

Willie was up and crashing dishes around in the kitchen to show his displeasure. He had learned of the solving of the murder from Priscilla as soon as he had got up and had come to the conclusion that Hamish had deliberately been keeping him out of the investigation.

Hamish went through to the kitchen. 'Look, Willie,' he said, 'most of the investigations took place in Strathbane, where I shouldn't have been. I couldnae risk getting the both of us in trouble.'

Willie was polishing dishes in the sink with a little mop. He hunched his shoulders and did not reply.

'It's no' as if you've shown any real interest in police work,' said Hamish, exasperated.

'I would ha' shown interest enough with any encouragement,' said Willie. 'You wanted all the kludos for yourself.'

'If you mean kudos, I did not. Take a walk, Willie I really need to talk to Priscilla in private. Take the morning off.' His voice grew wheedling. 'Mr Ferrari may not know the case is solved and he'd be right happy to hear about it.'

'I suppose it's ma duty to tell him,' said Willie reluctantly, 'seeing as how the auld man said you were trying to pin the murder on him because he's a foreigner.'

'Havers. But run along and tell him and don't come back until lunchtime.'

Willie removed his apron. 'I'll come back when I feel like it, *sir*.'

When he had gone, Hamish returned to Priscilla and said, 'That's got rid of him. Go and get the women here and I'll get that bag up from under the packing case.'

Hamish went up to the field and looked about to make sure no one was watching before he took the rocks out of the packing case and shoved it aside. He took the metal box out of the bag and then replaced it with some of the rocks.

Mrs Wellington, Jessie Currie and Angela Brodie were sitting in the living room when he returned.

'Do the police know?' asked Mrs Wellington, her face a muddy colour. 'Miss Halburton-Smythe would not tell us anything.'

'Only we know, us here in this room,' said Hamish. He opened the box. 'All the money Sean got from you will not be here, for I'm sure he spent a lot of it, but I'll leave it to you to divide up what's here, and Angela, you'd best put those packets of morphine back in the surgery.'

The three women looked at him without moving.

'Oh, the video,' said Hamish. 'Here it is.' He put a couple of fire-lighters on the fire, lit them and then threw the video on top of them.

Priscilla slid quietly out of the room.

Jessie, Angela and Mrs Wellington watched solemnly until the video disintegrated into a black molten mess.

'Now let's get to the money,' said Mrs Wellington with a return of her usual bossy manner.

Willie Lamont was met at the kitchen door by Lucia. She was carrying a sack of rubbish. 'I'll take that,' said Willie. 'You should not be carrying heavy loads like that.'

He walked round to the back of the restaurant and heaved the sack into the large rubbish container.

'You will make some lady a good husband, Weellie,' teased Lucia.

He turned and looked at her. The wind of the night before had calmed down to a light breeze. Tendrils of hair were blowing about her pretty face. He heaved a great sigh.

'Hamish Macbeth has the right of it,' he said sadly. 'I'm an auld woman, always fussing ower the housework. What woman would want a man like that?'

Lucia looked at him, wide-eyed. 'Do you

mean, if you were married, you would *still* be doing the housework?'

'Aye, that's a fact, Lucia. I'd always be there, fussing and cleaning.'

Her eyes began to glow. She thought back on her young life in the village in Italy with her seven little brothers and sisters, a life of perpetual cleaning and drudgery. She raised her red hands and looked at them, turning them this way and that, and then she put them gently on Willie's shoulders.

'You have never tried to kiss me, Weellie.'

He looked at her in surprise and then his eyes fell to that deliciously pouting mouth. He had dreamt of kissing Lucia, but always in some romantic setting, up on the heathery moors or out on a boat in the loch, but never had he imagined it as he was doing now, kissing her while the sea-gulls swooped and dived about the restaurant rubbish. He had never experienced anything like it. When he at last freed his mouth, he was trembling and tears were running down his cheeks.

'Don't make fun o' me,' he said hoarsely.

'I'll never make fun of you,' said Lucia, kissing the end of his pointed nose. 'Not even after we're married.'

'Married! You'd marry me? Oh, my heavens!'

'But you'd better go and see Mr Ferrari and get his permission. Will we live in the police station?'

'Will we, hell!' cried Willie. 'I've got a tidy bit put by and we'll get a nice house all to ourselves.'

They went in to see Mr Ferrari, who listened to them impassively and then said, 'Lucia, there are vegetables to prepare in the kitchen.'

Then he sat down at a restaurant table and waved a hand to indicate that Willie should sit opposite.

'Lucia is a good Catholic,' began Mr Ferrari.

'I'm a Roman Catholic myself,' said Willie.

'But I haven't seen you at mass.'

'A lapsed Catholic, but I can take it up agin,' said Willie eagerly.

'And will you be able to support her on a policeman's pay?'

Aye, I can that. I've got a good bit in the bank.'

'How much?'

'About fifty thousand pounds.'

'What! How did you get that?'

'I won one o' thae competitions in the news-papers.'

Mr Ferrari leaned back in his chair. 'I hear the murder has been solved by Hamish.'

'Aye,' said Willie bitterly, 'and he did his best tae keep me out of it. Wanted all the glory for hisself.'

'Do you like police work?'

Willie looked puzzled. 'I never really thought

about it, to tell you the truth. Everyone says it's a good job and you get respect.'

'But not from Hamish Macbeth. Would you expect Lucia to work once she was married?'

'Wouldn't dream of it,' said Willie.

The lizard eyes looked at him with calculation. 'You would be a boon to this restaurant of mine, Willie. Girls like Lucia I can get, but I am old and need someone to manage the place. Luigi and Giovanni would not mind. They are no good with orders and bookkeeping and know it. What would you say if I asked you to leave your job and come into business with me?'

Willie saw stretching out before him a life of endless cooking and cleaning and thought he might faint from excitement.

'Oh, that would be grand.'

'Then I suggest you tell that lanky drip of nothing called Hamish Macbeth the good news as soon as possible. He has done better for himself than he deserves.' Mr Ferrari leaned over and picked up a copy of the local newspaper. 'He is, I see, engaged to Priscilla Halburton-Smythe.'

'Oh, aye,' said Willie, 'I knew that was on the cards.'

Priscilla had arrived back at the police station with bottles of champagne which she had bought at Patel's. 'I thought we would all celebrate the end of the nightmare,' she said, popping a cork. 'Hamish, are you sure you didn't let slip about any of this to anyone other than us?'

'Of course not. Why?'

'Mr Patel kept shaking my hand and saying, "Congratulations."'

'He probably knows you were there with me when we caught Cheryl,' said Hamish.

'That must be it,' said Priscilla doubtfully.

Nessie Currie erupted into the room and glared at her sister. 'So this is where ye are!' she cried. 'And drinking champagne like the veriest whore. Shame on ye. Are ye not in enough trouble as it is? Are ye . . .?'

Jessie smiled mistily at her sister over the rim of her champagne glass as Mrs Wellington interrupted Nessie's tirade with a booming cry of 'Hamish has burnt the video and you've got most of your money back.'

Nessie sank down slowly into a chair and heard the whole story. 'Oh, my,' she said weakly, 'and here's me ranting and raving. And of course there's every reason why we should be drinking champagne on this happy day, Miss Halburton-Smythe. Yes, I'll hae a glass and drink to your health.'

'Thank you,' said Priscilla in surprise.

Angela smiled teasingly at Hamish. She already looked years younger. 'John always said you'd never do it, Hamish, but I was sure you would.'

'I'm surprised at Dr Brodie,' said Hamish. 'I haff solved the murders afore.'

'Oh, not *that*. When is it to be?'

'When's what?'

'Why, your wedding!'

'What wedding?' howled Hamish.

'It's in the *Gazette* this morning,' said Angela, puzzled. 'You and Priscilla.'

'Oh, my poor father,' said Priscilla weakly. 'He'll have a stroke.'

'You mean,' said Angela, her face falling, 'that you haven't ... that you didn't know anything about it?'

'Not a thing.'

The phone rang in the police station office. Hamish went to answer it. It was Superintendent Peter Daviot from Strathbane. 'Well done, Hamish,' he cried.

'Thank you,' said Hamish modestly. 'I was just doing my job.'

'Not your job, man, your engagement. Terrific news. My wife's going out to look for an engagement present for you.'

'But –'

'Not another word, you sly dog!'

And the superintendent rang off.

'Don't worry, Hamish,' came Priscilla's voice from next to him. 'We'll get the paper to print an apology.'

He twisted his head and looked up at her. She looked amused, cool and beautiful . . . and distant.

With one abrupt movement, he pushed back his chair, and reaching up an arm, jerked her down on to his knees and began to kiss her, dizzy with emotion, fatigue, whisky and champagne.

The phone began to ring again but both ignored it. Willie walked in and picked it up. 'Oh, it's yerself, Mrs Macbeth,' he said to Hamish's mother. 'Yes, that's right. Well, himself is tied up at the moment. I'll get him to ring back.'

He shook his head over the entwined couple and went out.

'Who was that?' murmured Priscilla against Hamish's lips.

'Don't know and don't care. Kiss me again.'

'Is this a proposal, Hamish?'

'Aye.'

'Well, take your hand out of my brassiere and listen to me for a moment.'

Hamish gave her a wounded look. 'You're not going to be *sensible*, are you?'

'Yes, I am. I don't think I trust you, Hamish. I love you but I don't trust you. I think you've got too much of an eye for the ladies.'

'But I'm proposing to *you*, Priscilla.'

'Okay, but just an engagement, a *long* engagement.'

'Anything you say.'

'Do you love me?'

'I've been trying not to for years.'

'Now kiss me again.'

Willie arrived back at the police station. It was as quiet as the grave. He walked into the living room and scowled at the mess of dirty glasses and empty champagne bottles. Then he saw a note addressed to himself pinned on Hamish's bedroom door. He took it down and opened it. It said, 'Tell everyone I have gone out. Must get some sleep. Hamish.'

But Willie wanted to tell Hamish that he was leaving, so he gently opened Hamish's bedroom door. Hamish and Priscilla were lying together on Hamish's narrow bed. They were both fast asleep. They were lying on top of the bedclothes, fully dressed with all their clothes, and with Towser at their feet, but Willie blushed furiously and quickly shut the door again.

Then he brightened as he turned and looked around the messy room. He would give the police station one last good clean-up.

Mr Wellington returned home that evening after a round of visits to the old and sick in the parish. He expected his wife to be asleep. He had complained to Dr Brodie about the number of sleeping pills she was taking, but Dr Brodie said that she must be getting them from another doctor, possibly in Strathbane. To his surprise, he smelled cooking, delicious cooking. It seemed he had been having squalid cold meals for ages.

'Ah, there you are,' said his wife briskly as he entered the large manse kitchen. 'Sit down. Dinner's nearly ready. Steak-and-kidney pie, mashed potatoes and Brussels sprouts, and make sure you eat all your greens, dear. You've been looking peaky of late.'

'Yes, my love,' said the minister happily.

'Oh, by the way, that money that was missing from the Mothers' Union turned up again. It was left in the church hall on the kitchen counter . . . no note, no anything. We're all quite sure it was a passing tramp or someone like that who had a fit of conscience and put it back.'

Mrs Wellington briskly and efficiently took a golden-crusted steak-and-kidney pie out of the oven.

Mr Wellington clasped his hands and bowed his head. 'Thank you, God,' he said.

'Why, you're praying,' cried Mrs Wellington.

'Why, so I am,' said the minister.

Dr Brodie could not quite put his finger on it but he knew that things had changed the minute he opened the door and walked into his house. He went into the kitchen. His wife was sitting behind a pile of textbooks as usual, but there seemed to be a lightness in the very air.

'I feel a bit daft,' he said, sitting down. 'I was checking the drugs cabinet and I found those missing packets of morphine. They'd got stuck inside a packet of something else. I should call Hamish.'

Angela smiled at him. 'Leave it till tomorrow. I thought we would eat out tonight. I've booked a table at the Napoli.'

'Great idea. Why don't you wear one of your new dresses?'

'I haven't got them.'

'What!'

'I sold them down in Inverness. That's where I've been today,' lied Angela. 'I got most of the money back.'

'Well, good for you. I didn't know you could get any money at all for second-hand clothes.'

'These were models.'

'I don't know anything about women's clothes, but if it means dinner at the Napoli, then that's grand.'

Hamish woke early in the evening and stretched out and felt around for Priscilla. But she had gone. He groaned and sat up and went through to the police office. There was a long string of messages and demands to call back. He began to work his way through them, starting with his mother, and so down to Jimmy Anderson.

'Thought you'd like to know,' said Anderson, 'that we got that pop band to crack and they admitted covering up for Cheryl.'

'That's grand.'

'The bad news is that I visited Blair in hospital. He's made a complete recovery, but he's been told to stay off the booze and go to Alcoholics Anonymous.'

'God grant them the serenity when Blair turns up, cursing and blinding, at one o' their meetings,' said Hamish with feeling.

'Can you imagine what he'll be like sober?' demanded Anderson peevishly. 'The only time that man's human is when he's drunk. Talking about getting drunk, are you celebrating your engagement?'

'I plan to. I've lost her for the moment.'

'Good luck tae ye. Her father's probably taking a horsewhip to her right now. What d'ye think o' Willie leaving the force?'

'I didn't know. He didn't tell me.'

'He's going into the restaurant business. The trouble is we cannae find a copper at the moment to replace him, so you're on your own again.'

Bliss, thought Hamish, after he had rung off. Sheer bliss.

He picked up the phone again and rang the castle and with bad luck got Priscilla's father on the other end. In a mild voice, he asked to speak to Priscilla.

'Before I get my daughter,' said the colonel in a low, quiet voice, quite unlike his usual blustering tones, 'if you think you are going to marry her, you've got another think coming. She will never marry you, Hamish Macbeth, and I will do my best to stop you. I am warning you.'

'So I'm warned,' snapped Hamish. 'Just get her.'

When Priscilla answered, she said hurriedly, 'Meet me at the Napoli in about ten minutes. I've got to get out of here.'

'That bad?'

'Worse. He's gone all quiet and sinister and Mummy keeps crying and saying I'm ruining my life.'

'They'll get used to it,' said Hamish heartlessly.

The Napoli was crowded. Willie and Lucia were seated at the best table with Mr Ferrari, all toasting each other with Asti Spumanti. Before Hamish could join Priscilla, Mr Ferrari waved him over. 'So what do you think about Willie managing this business for me?'

'Grand,' said Hamish, shaking Willie's hand. 'Just grand. All the best.'

Mr Ferrari gave him a baffled look. 'You are pleased to be losing such a good officer?'

'I'm pleased because he's happy,' said Hamish.

Mr Ferrari gave a sudden amused shrug. 'You are a man of many surprises, Hamish.'

Hamish threaded his way through the tables towards Priscilla, accepting the congratulations of the locals.

She was wearing a slim low-cut silk dress with a delicate necklace of small emeralds set in gold. Her face was calm and beautiful.

He felt a momentary pang of unease. This was the beauty he was going to share his policestation life with! It seemed incredible.

'I know,' said Priscilla sympathetically, although he had not spoken, 'it takes some getting used to.'

'It's been quite a day,' said Hamish awkwardly. He felt desperately shy of her for the first time.

He fought to find a topic of conversation and then remembered that Sean's mother was due to arrive on the following day and that Ian Chisholm at the garage had promised to make her an offer for the bus. When he had exhausted that topic of conversation and ordered the meal, he sat in a miserable silence.

Priscilla stood up with one graceful fluid movement, came round the table and kissed him full on the mouth.

'Better?' she asked as she sat down again.

Hamish's face suddenly lit up with sheer happiness.

'Better? I'm in heaven!'

The next day dawned fine and warm. Hamish dealt with the painful business of Mrs Gourlay, who turned out to be a small, quiet, faded lady, not in the least like her flamboyant son.

When it was all over, he went to the henhouse and dragged an old deck-chair out, cleaned it and put it on the patch of grass in front of the police station and stretched out on it.

'Quite like old times. I say quite like old times,' came a familiar voice from the hedge.

Hamish straightened up and found the Currie sisters looking at him. But suddenly, as he looked at Jessie, he had an embarrassing picture of how she had looked naked on that video and somehow that picture seemed to have transferred itself in that moment from his mind to Jessie's.

She blushed deep red, gave a strangled squawk, and sped off, dragging her sister after her.

Hamish lay back in his deck-chair and grinned.

If you enjoyed *Death of a Travelling Man*, read
on for the first chapter of the next book in the
Hamish Macbeth series . . .

DEATH OF A
CHARMING
MAN

Chapter One

*The First Blast of the Trumpet Against the
Monstrous Regiment of Women.*
                                    – John Knox

Hamish Macbeth opened the curtains of his
bedroom window, scratched his chest lazily
and looked out at the loch. It was a bleached
sort of day, the high milky-white cloud with
the sun behind it draining colour from the
loch, from the surrounding hills, as if the village of Lochdubh were in some art film,
changing from colour to black and white. He
opened the window and a gust of warm damp
air blew in along with a cloud of stinging
midges, those Highland mosquitoes. He
slammed the window again and turned and
looked at his rumpled bed. There had been no
crime for months, no villains to engage the
attentions of Police Sergeant Macbeth. There
was, therefore, no reason why he could not

crawl back into that bed and dream another hour away.

And then he heard it ... faint sounds of scrubbing from the kitchen.

Priscilla!

The sweetness of his unofficial engagement to Priscilla Halburton-Smythe, daughter of a local hotelier and landowner, was fast fading. Cool Priscilla would never deliver herself of such a trite saying as 'I am making a man of you, Hamish Macbeth,' but that, thought Hamish gloomily, was what she was trying to do. He did not want to be made a man of, he wanted to slouch around the village, gossiping, poaching, and free-loading as he had always done in the tranquil days before his engagement.

There came a grinding of wheels outside, the slamming of doors, and then Priscilla's voice, 'Oh, good. Bring it right in here.'

Bring what?

He opened the bedroom door and ambled into the kitchen. Where his wood-burning stove had stood, there was a blank space. Two men in uniforms of the Hydro-Electric Board were carrying in a gleaming new electric cooker.

'Whit's this?' demanded Hamish sharply.

Priscilla flashed him a smile. 'Oh, Hamish, you lazy thing. It was to be a surprise. I've got

214

rid of that nasty old cooker of yours and bought a new electric one. Surprise!'

Hampered by Highland politeness, Hamish stifled his cry that he wanted his old stove back and mumbled, 'Thank you. You should-nae hae done it.'

'Miss Halburton-Smythe!' boomed a voice from the doorway and in lumbered the tweedy figure of Mrs Wellington, the minister's wife. 'I came to see the new cooker,' she said. 'My, isn't that grand. You're a lucky man, Hamish Macbeth.'

Hamish gave a smile which was more like a rictus and backed off. 'Aye, chust grand. If you ladies will excuse me, I'll wash and shave.'

He went into the newly painted bathroom and looked bleakly at the shower unit over the bath. 'Much more hygenic, Hamish. You spend too much time wallowing in the bath,' echoed Priscilla's voice in his head.

He washed and shaved at the handbasin, taking a childish pleasure in deciding to have neither shower nor bath. He went back to the bedroom and put on his regulation shirt and trousers and cap. Then he opened the bedroom window and climbed out, feeling a guilty sense of freedom. Towser, his mongrel dog, came bounding around the side of the house to join him. He set off along the waterfront with the dog at his heels. He had forgotten his stick of repellent but was reluctant to go back and fetch it, so he went into Patel's, the general store, and bought a stick. Jessie and Nessie Currie, the spinster sisters, were buying groceries.

'I heard you had the new cooker,' said Jessie. 'The new cooker.' She had an irritating habit of repeating everything.

'You're the lucky man,' said Nessie. 'We wass just saying the other day, a fine young woman like Miss Halburton-Smythe is mair than you deserve.'

'Be the making of you, the making of you,' said Jessie.

Hamish smiled weakly and retreated.

He went along and sat on the harbour wall and watched the fishing boats bobbing at anchor. There was something about him, he decided, pushing back his cap and scratching his red hair, which brought out the cleaning beast in people. He had successfully rid himself of Willie Lamont, his police constable, now working at the Italian restaurant, after Willie had nearly driven him mad with his cleaning. The first few heady days of his unofficial engagement to Priscilla had not lasted very long. At first it seemed right that she should start to reorganize the police station, considering she was going to live there. It had to be admitted that the station did need a good clean. But every day? And then she had decided he was not eating properly, and to

Hamish's mind nourishing meals meant boring meals, and the more nourishing meals he received from Priscilla's fair hands, the more he thought of going down to Inverness for the day and stuffing himself with junk food. He felt disloyal, but he could not also help feeling rather wistful as he remembered the days when his life had been his own. He remembered reading a letter in an agony column from a 'distressed' housewife in which she had complained her husband did not give her enough 'space' and he had thought then, cynically, that the woman had little to complain about. Now he knew what she felt. For not only was Priscilla always underfoot, banging pots and pans, but the ladies of the village had taken to calling, and the police station was full of the sound of female voices, all praising Priscilla's improvements. He was sure the police station would be full of them for the rest of the day. A new electric cooker in Lochdubh was the equivalent of a guest appearance by Madonna anywhere else.

He slid down off the wall and headed back along the waterfront and up out of the village, with Towser loping at his heels. Hamish had decided to go to the Tommel Castle Hotel, now run by Priscilla's father, to see if Mr Johnston, the manager, would give him a cup of coffee. Priscilla's home seemed to be the one place these days where he was sure he would not run into her.

Mr Johnston was in his office. He smiled when he saw Hamish and nodded towards the coffee percolator in the corner. 'Help yourself, Hamish. It's a long time since you've come mooching around. Where's Priscilla?'

'Herself has chust bought me the new cooker,' said Hamish over his shoulder as he poured a mug of coffee. Mr Johnston knew of old that Hamish's accent became more sibilant when the police sergeant was upset.

'Oh, aye,' said the hotel manager, eyeing the rigidity of Hamish's thin back. 'Well, that's marriage for ye. Nothing like the ladies for getting life sorted out.'

'I'm a lucky man,' said Hamish repressively. He never discussed Priscilla with anyone. He often wondered if there was anyone he could discuss her with, even if he had wanted to. Everyone, particularly his own mother, kept telling him how lucky he was.

'You might not be seeing so much of her in the next week or two,' said Mr Johnston.

'And why is that?' Hamish sat down on the opposite side of the desk and sipped his coffee.

'Hotel's going to be full up. The maids keep going off work with one excuse or the other. So you won't be seeing much of her, like I said. You need a crime to keep you going.'

'I don't get bored,' said Hamish mildly. 'I am not looking for the crime to keep me amused.'

The hotel manager looked at the tall gangling policeman with affection. 'I often wonder why you ever bothered to join the police force, Hamish. Why not jist be a Highland layabout, draw the dole, poach a bit?'

'Oh, the police suits me chust fine. Also, if I had the big crime here again, they might send me an assistant and I could not be doing with being scrubbed out o' house and home.'

'So what are you doing here when you ought to be wi' your sweetie? A rare hand with the scrubbing brush is our Priscilla, talking about being scrubbed out.'

Hamish looked at him blankly and Mr Johnston suddenly felt he had been impertinent. 'Well, I've a wee bit o' gossip for you,' he said hurriedly. 'Drim is on your beat, isn't it?'

'Aye, but nothing's ever happened there and never will. It must be the dullest place in the British Isles.'

'Oh, but something has happened. Beauty's come to Drim and it ain't a lassie but a fellow. Folks say he's like a film star.'

'What brings him to a place like Drim?'

'God knows. Jist strolled into the village one day, bought a wee bit of a croft house and started doing it up. Posh chap. English.'

'Oh, one o' them.'

'Aye, he'll play at being a villager for a bit and talk about the simple life and then one winter up here will send him packing.'

'The winters aren't so bad.'

'I amnae talking about the weather, Hamish. I'm talking about that shut-down feeling that happens up here in the winter where you sit and think the rest of the world has gone off somewhere to have a party, leaving you alone in a black wilderness.'

'I don't feel like that.'

'No? Well, I suppose it's because I'm from the city,' said Mr Johnston, who came from Glasgow.

'I might take a look over at Drim and pay a visit to this fellow,' said Hamish. 'Any chance of borrowing one of the hotel cars?'

'What's happened to the police Land Rover?'

Hamish shifted awkwardly. 'It's down at the police station. I walked here. Chust wanted to save myself the walk back.'

'Well, if you're not going to have it away too long,' said Mr Johnston, stopping himself in time from pointing out that when Hamish returned the car, he would still have to walk back to Lochdubh. He opened the desk drawer and fished out a set of car keys. 'Take the Volvo. But don't keep it out all day. The new guests will be arriving. I'll just give Priscilla a ring and tell her she'd better be here to welcome them.'

Hamish took the keys and strolled off. As he drove out on the road to Drim, he felt as if he were on holiday, as if he were driving away from the monstrous regiment of women, the rule of women as John Knox had meant, the one particular woman in his life who was hell-bent on making a successful man of him. Priscilla had determinedly set out to make friends with the wife of Chief Superintendent Peter Daviot. Hamish knew Priscilla wanted him to be promoted higher. But promotion meant living in Strathbane, promotion meant exams, promotion meant becoming a detective and never being allowed back to Lochdubh again. He shoved his worried thoughts firmly to the back of his mind.

The wind was rising and tearing the milky clouds into ragged wisps. The sun shone fitfully down, the heather blazed purple along the flanks of the mountains, and as he gained the crest of a hill he looked down across a breath-taking expanse of mountain and moorland, with the tarns of Sutherland gleaming sapphire-blue among the heather where the clumsy grouse stumbled, flapped, and rose before the swift feet of a herd of deer.

He concentrated his mind on wondering what had brought this Adonis to a place like Drim.

Drim was a peculiar place at the end of a thin sea loch on a flat piece of land surrounded by towering black mountains. The loch itself was black, a corridor of a loch between the high walls of the mountains where little grew among the scree and black rock but stunted bushes. The only access to Drim, unless one was foolhardy enough to brave a trip by sea, was by a narrow one track road over the hills from the east. The village was a huddle of houses with a church, a community hall, a general store, but no police station. The village was policed from Lochdubh by Hamish Macbeth, although the villagers hardly ever saw him. There had never been any crime in Drim, not even drunkenness, for there was no pub, and no alcohol for sale.

He parked the car and went into the general store run by a giant of a man called Jock Kennedy. 'Hamish,' said Jock, 'have not seen you in ages. What iss bringing you to us?'

'Just curiosity,' said Hamish. 'I hear you've got an incomer.'

'Oh, aye. Peter Hynd. Nice young man. Bought that old croft house o' Geordie Black's up above the village. Putting in his own drains. Old Geordie just used a hut out the back for a toilet and there wasnae a bathroom, old Geordie not believing in washing all ower except for funerals and weddings.'

'Geordie's dead then?'

'Aye, died six month ago, and his daughter sold the house. She was as surprised as anyone, I am telling you, when this young fellow offered her the money for it. She thocht it would be lying there until it fell to bits.'

'I might just go and hae a wee word with him,' said Hamish. He bought a bottle of fizzy lemonade and two sausage rolls and ate and drank, sitting outside on a bench in front of the shop. Priscilla, he thought with a stab of guilt, would no doubt have prepared a nourishing lunch for him, brown rice and something or other. He should have phoned her.

The loch was only a few yards away, its black waters sucking at the oily stones on the beach. Everything was very quiet and still. The mountains shut out the wind and shut out most of the light. A grim, sad place. What on earth was a beautiful young Englishman doing here?

The village consisted of several cottages grouped about the store. It was a Highland village that time had forgotten. The only new building was the ugly square community hall with its tin roof, its walls painted acid-sulphurous yellow. Behind the hall was the church, a small stone building with a Celtic cross at one end of the roof and an iron bell at the other. Hamish realized with surprise that although he knew Jock Kennedy, he hardly knew anyone else in this odd village to speak to. He rose and stretched and gave the last of one of his sausage rolls to Towser and then set out for Peter Hynd's cottage.

He heard the sounds of pick on rock as he approached. It was an ugly little grey cottage with a corrugated-iron roof. A new fence had been put around a weedy garden where no flowers grew. He walked round the cottage towards the sound of the pick and there, down a trench, working industriously, stripped to the waist, was the most beautiful man Hamish had ever seen. He stopped his work, put down the pick, scrambled nimbly out of the trench and stood looking at Hamish, his hands on his hips.

Peter Hynd was about five feet ten inches in height. His face and body were lightly tanned a golden brown. His figure was slim and well-muscled. He had golden hair which curled on his head like a cap. He had high cheek-bones and golden-brown eyes framed with thick lashes. His mouth was firm and well-shaped and his neck was the kind of neck that classical sculptors dream about.

'Hello,' he said. 'Is this visit official?'

'No,' said Hamish, 'Just a friendly call.'

Peter smiled suddenly and Hamish blinked as though before a sudden burst of sunlight. That smile illuminated the young man's face with a radiance. 'You'd better come indoors,' said Peter, 'and have something. Tea or coffee?'

'Coffee would be chust fine,' said Hamish, feeling suddenly shy.

Peter took a checked shirt off a nail on the

fence and put it on. His accent was light, pleasant, upper-class but totally without drawl or affectation.

Hamish followed him into the house, ducking his head as he did so, for the doorway was low. The cottage was in the usual old-fashioned croft-house pattern, living room with a fire for cooking on to one side and parlour to the other. Peter had transformed the living room into a sort of temporary kitchen, with a counter along one side with shelves containing dishes, and pots and pans above it. In the centre of the room was a scrubbed kitchen table surrounded by high-backed chairs. Peter put a kettle on a camping stove at the edge of the table. 'I used that old kettle on the chain over the fire when I first arrived,' he said with a grin, 'but it took ages to boil. The peat around here doesn't give out much heat. Milk and sugar?'

'Just black,' said Hamish, beginning to feel more at ease.

'I'm building a kitchen at the back,' said Peter, taking down two mugs.

'What are you doing in the garden?' asked Hamish.

'Digging drains and a cesspool. I plan to have a flushing toilet and a bathroom. You've no idea what it's like when you want a pee in the middle of the night and have to go out to that hut in the garden.'

'You might find it difficult to get help,' said Hamish. 'The locals can be a bit standoffish.'

Peter looked surprised. 'On the contrary, I've had more offers of help than I can cope with. People are very kind. I didn't know we had a policeman.'

'You don't. I'm over at Lochdubh. This is part of my beat.'

'Much crime?'

'Verra quiet, I'm glad to say.'

'Macbeth, Macbeth. That rings a bell. Oh, I know. You've been involved in some murder cases up here.'

'Yes, but I am hoping neffer to be involved in another. Thank you for the coffee.'

Peter sat down opposite Hamish and stretched like a cat. A good thing there were no young women in Drim, thought Hamish, with this heart-breaker around.

'Do you plan to stay here?' he asked curiously.

'Yes, why not?'

'But you're a young man. There's nothing for you here.'

'On the contrary, I think I've found what I'm looking for.'

'That being?'

There was a slight hesitation. Hamish shivered suddenly. 'Tranquillity,' said Peter vaguely. 'Building things, working with my hands.'

Hamish finished his coffee and got up to leave.

'Come again,' said Peter and again there was that blinding smile.

Hamish smiled back. 'Aye, I will that, and maybe next time I'll give you a hand.'

Hamish walked away from the cottage still smiling, but as he reached the car parked in the village his smile faded. He gave himself a little shake. There was no doubt that Peter Hynd possessed great charm. But out of his orbit, Hamish found himself almost disliking the man, almost afraid of him, and wondered why. With a little sigh he opened the passenger door for Towser to leap in, before getting into the driver's seat.

His spirits lifted when he drove up the hill out of Drim and into the sunshine. There was no need to go back to Drim for some time, no need at all.

He parked the hotel car in the forecourt of Tommel Castle and then walked into the hotel and handed the keys to Mr Johnston.

'Priscilla's back,' said the hotel manager. 'Will I let her know you're here?'

'No, no,' said Hamish. 'I've got my chores to do. I'll phone her later.'

He hurried off. Five minutes later Priscilla walked into the hotel office. 'Someone told me they had seen Hamish and Towser walking off,' she said.

'Aye, he said he couldnae wait. He had chores to do.'

'I wonder what those could be,' said Priscilla cynically. 'All he's got to do is put the dinner I left him in his new oven. Did he tell you about the electric cooker?'

'Yes, he did mention it. Did you ask him if he wanted a new cooker?'

'No, why? There was no reason to. That old stove was a disgrace.'

'I think he liked it,' said Mr Johnston cautiously. 'Cosy in the winter.'

'He's got central heating now.'

'Aye, but there's nothing like a real fire. You won't change Hamish, Priscilla.'

'I am not trying to change him,' snapped Priscilla. 'You forget, I'm going to have to live in that police station myself.'

'Oh, well, suit yourself.'

'In fact, I might just run down there. I left the instruction booklet for the new cooker on the table, but you know Hamish.'

'Aye, he's a grown man and not a bairn.'

Priscilla fidgeted nervously with a pencil on the desk. 'Nonetheless, I'll just go and see how he's doing.'

Mr Johnston shook his head sadly after she had left. It was as if the usually cool and calm Priscilla had taken up a cause and that cause was the advancement of Hamish Macbeth.

Priscilla pulled up outside the police station. Dr Brodie was walking past and raised his cap. The doctor was one of the few people in the village opposed to the forthcoming marriage of Hamish Macbeth and Priscilla Halburton-Smythe. He saw over Priscilla's shoulder as she got out of her car the approaching figure of Hamish at the far end of the waterfront. Priscilla must have passed him on the road without seeing him.

'If you're looking for Hamish,' said Dr Brodie, 'he's gone off to see Angus Macdonald.'

'That old fraud!'

'He's been feeling poorly.'

Priscilla opened her car door again. 'I may as well rescue him before Angus pretends to tell his future.'

She drove off, swinging the car round.

That was childish of me, thought the doctor. I was only trying to give Hamish a break, but she's bound to see him.

But as he looked along the waterfront, there was no sign of Hamish. Priscilla's car sped out of view. Then Hamish reappeared. Dr Brodie grinned. Hamish must have dived for cover. Priscilla should be marrying one of her own kind, he thought, old-fashioned snobbery mixing with common sense.

Angus Macdonald had gained a certain fame as a seer. Priscilla thought he was a shrewd old man who listened to all the village gossip and made his predictions accordingly.

When she drove up it was to see the old man working in his garden. He waved to her and beckoned.

She went forward reluctantly. The Land Rover had been outside the police station. Hamish surely would not have bothered walking.

'Dr Brodie said you were not feeling well,' said Priscilla. 'Where's Hamish?'

'Why should he say that? I havenae seen Hamish.'

'I'd better be getting back.'

'Och, stay a minute and give an auld man the pleasure of your company.'

Priscilla followed the seer into his cottage, noticing with irritation that he was putting the kettle on the peat fire to boil. With the money he conned out of people, she thought, he could well afford to buy something modern.

But she politely asked after his health and learned to her increasing irritation that it was 'neffer better.'

Angus settled down finally over the teapot and asked her a lot of searching questions about people in the village. 'I thought you were a seer,' said Priscilla finally and impatiently. 'You are supposed to know all this by just sitting on your backside and dreaming.'

'I see things all right.' Angus Macdonald was a tall, thin man in his sixties. He had a thick head of white hair and a craggy face with an enormous beak of a nose. He smiled at Priscilla and said, 'I see your future.' His voice had taken on an odd crooning note. Priscilla, despite herself, felt hypnotized. 'You will not marry Macbeth. A beautiful man will come between you.'

Priscilla burst out laughing. 'Oh, Angus, *honestly*. There is nothing homosexual about Hamish.'

'I wisnae saying that. I see a beautiful young man and he's going to come between you two.'

Priscilla picked up her handbag. 'I've no intention of being unfaithful to Hamish either. Beautiful young man, indeed.'

She drove down to the police station, but as she was raising her hand to knock at the kitchen door, she heard the sound of masculine laughter coming from inside. She walked around the back of the house and glanced in the kitchen window. Hamish and Dr Brodie were sitting at the kitchen table, an open whisky bottle in front of them. Hamish appeared more relaxed and amused than Priscilla had seen him look for some time.

She walked away and got back in the car. Surely Dr Brodie could not have been deliberately lying to her about Angus. But she felt reluctant to go in there and face him with it. Besides, the new guests would be arriving about now at the hotel. She would feel more like her old self when she got down to work.

231

She always felt better these days when she was working.

When she arrived at the hotel, Mr Johnston popped his head outside the office door and said, 'Thon Mrs Daviot's on the line for you.'

Priscilla brightened. The Chief Superintendent's wife. 'Hello, Mrs Daviot,' she said.

'Now didn't I tell you to call me Susan?' said Mrs Daviot coyly. 'Ai have been thinking, Priscilla, dear, that there are some vairy nice houses around Strathbane. If Hamish got a promotion, you'd need to live here. It wouldn't do any hairm to look at just a few of them.'

'I suppose not,' said Priscilla cautiously. 'But Hamish might not like it. He's set on staying in Lochdubh.'

'All that young man needs is a push,' said Mrs Daviot. 'Once you get him out of Lochdubh, he'll forget the place existed.'

CRIME AND THRILLER FAN?

CHECK OUT THECRIMEVAULT.COM

The online home of
exceptional crime fiction

KEEP YOURSELF IN SUSPENSE

Sign up to our newsletter for regular recommendations,
competitions and exclusives at www.thecrimevault.com/connect

Follow us on twitter for all the latest news @TheCrimeVault